I0722716

The River Blade

Previous Books
The Blood Within the Stone 9781922200822
The Forked Path 9781925652390
A Flame of Song 9781922311450

The River Blade

T.R. Thompson

ROUNDFIRE
BOOKS

London, UK
Washington, DC, USA

CollectiveInk

First published by Roundfire Books, 2025
Roundfire Books is an imprint of Collective Ink Ltd.,
Unit 11, Shepperton House, 89 Shepperton Road, London, N1 3DF
office@collectiveinkbooks.com
www.collectiveinkbooks.com
www.roundfire-books.com

For distributor details and how to order please visit the 'Ordering' section on our website.

Text copyright: T.R. Thompson 2024

ISBN: 978 1 80341 859 9
978 1 80341 864 3 (ebook)
Library of Congress Control Number: 2024936807

All rights reserved. Except for brief quotations in critical articles or reviews, no part of this book may be reproduced in any manner without prior written permission from the publishers.

The rights of T.R. Thompson as author have been asserted in accordance with the Copyright, Designs and Patents Act 1988.

A CIP catalogue record for this book is available from the British Library.

Design: Lapiz Digital Services

We operate a distinctive and ethical publishing philosophy in all areas of our business, from our global network of authors to production and worldwide distribution.

*The most merciful thing in the world, I think, is the inability
of the human mind to correlate all its contents. We live on a
placid island of ignorance in the midst of black seas of infinity,
and it was not meant that we should voyage far.*
H.P. Lovecraft, *The Call of Cthulhu*

Part 1

A virus begins to spread in the waters of the River, a strange duo embarks on an investigation, a potential saviour begins to discover her potential, and God shuffles his feet.

Prologue

The car zipped through the raindrops, fifty feet in the air, seeming to wait till the last microsecond before swerving to avoid the assorted billboards and rooftops that reached up towards it. The autopilot didn't need to see the obstacles to know they were there. Kane let it do the driving, it had far better reactions than he did anyway. Besides, he was lost in his own world, with its own distractions.

He sat in the driver's seat; the cable leading from just behind his ear to the car input. The data port. Some still called them radios, but they were so much more. On the other side of the port Kane was sitting around a campfire with friends on a warm summer night, drinking cold beer and smoking good weed. Looking up at the stars. There wasn't a cloud in the sky in his world.

In reality he sat in the car seat with a slack, dazed expression on his face. His eyes were open and glazed over. He was fifteen minutes away from where she'd last been seen, and it was best to spend what time he could relaxing.

Besides, what was there to look at out there? Darkness and rain, the usual story outside the Grid. And if he dared get close enough to street level a lot of other, nastier things might flicker across his headlights. The car knew not to get too low though. It would stay out of range of the hookers.

Why had she come out here? Outside of the safety of the central hub that was the Grid? What had driven her to run into the dark, to float away on the River, away from everything they had, everything everyone who wasn't completely crazy had. What had he done that was so wrong?

Music began to leak out of the radio and slowly increased in volume as if trying to make itself noticed. It was a simple tune, something easily remembered. Something that would stay with you.

Kane was lying back on the sand when one of his friends started to hum softly. Then another. When he sat up everyone around the campfire was humming along, staring at him with blank eyes. Then they all disappeared.

He shook his head to clear the last of the images from his mind and found himself back in the car. The fucking port was playing up. Oh well, he could have it looked at later, he wasn't far away now.

He yanked the cable out from behind his ear and peered out the windows to see if he could recognise anything. It took him a couple of seconds to realise the song was still in the air.

At first, he simply couldn't understand what was happening. He'd pulled out the jack, where was this sound coming from if not from there? The car didn't have speakers, there was no need when every passenger could simply jack straight into their skull. What the fuck was going on?

Kane stared down at the dashboard and punched the radio's face. The song only seemed to get louder. It brushed the back of his neck and made the hairs stand on end.

The blood in his face drained away and he began to feel ill. It was as if the music itself was sucking it out of him, pumping it back up into his brain, overloading it. He felt something tickle his ankle and looked down at the car floor.

Bugs. It was crawling with bugs. Cockroaches, caterpillars, spiders, swarming all over the floor, all over his feet, crawling up his legs. Kane yanked his feet up to the seat with a yelp, but the moving blanket seemed to rise with them.

They slithered over his lap, over his hands and chest. He shook uncontrollably and tried to pull himself up out of the safety belt. He could feel tiny legs tickling his throat.

He lost control and kicked and writhed in utter panic. The car dipped dramatically as he knocked the autopilot off, then began a lazy dive into the closest building. By the time the bugs were inside him the car had hit.

An explosion cracked across the area as the machine disintegrated in a pyre of flame. It drowned out every other sound, even the song which slowly faded out and wandered away.

There's no problem a drink can't fix. That's why he was here, in the same seat, in the same bar. This bar was his home now. An island between two worlds, it was the one place where everything was still possible. It was his place to dream.

Adlai looked around, scanning the room. There were two others slumped over their drinks in the corner and a lone bartender needlessly polishing glasses. Otherwise, the joint was empty.

Of course it was.

He motioned with his finger. The bartender reached under the bar and came back up with a straight bourbon in an old-fashioned glass. He slid it across with a nod.

Adlai took his drink and stared up at the small black window in front of him. As he sipped the burn ran down his throat and turned into a heat that spread through his cells, making his whole body tingle. That wasn't a good sign. When your body starts crying out for its hit like that it means something.

Means it's time for another drink.

He looked up but there was already another full one sitting in front of him.

Outside it was streaming rain, a steady downpour through the darkness. Just like yesterday and the day before that. Just like tomorrow would be.

He looked down at his drink again and moved his hand towards it. An inch from the glass he stopped and switched his brain on for the first time in days, weeks perhaps. The glass slid across the bar into his palm as if drawn by a magnet. No one else noticed, but it brought a small smile to his lips.

As he sat back and got on with drinking, he stared out the window and tried to recall if he'd ended up here because he was trying to remember or trying to forget. He could never be sure anymore. Not with all he had done, all that he knew.

He was riddled with rich seams of guilt. He was there to sink down into the mine and dredge them up, polish them into hard, shining jewels.

He stared out the window and began to dream.

***

Cass hunched down behind the broken chimney and waited for the familiar hum of the car to come into range. She didn't hear it; she didn't hear anything anymore, but she could feel it, track its vibration in her stomach. This was the first target they'd seen off-Grid in months. They couldn't afford to let it get away.

She closed her eyes and focused her mind. The outside world shut down to a sheet of black, a tiny pin prick of white light in the centre. Just worry about the shot. Make it straight, make it true, make it clean.

Across the alley on the opposite rooftop the rest of the gang waited for her signal. They knew from experience to trust her tuned instincts, follow her lead. How much things had changed from that moment, months ago now, when they'd first found her wandering alone through the dark laneways. When he'd first saved her.

Cass smiled to herself and felt the rain drip down off her curved lips. Quarters had grabbed her from behind and held her quiet and close to save her life. She'd like to see him try that now.

The hum was closer now. She fingered her crossbow and arranged the plan in her mind. As the car passed over the top of them, flying too low of course, not expecting anything this far off-Grid, they would each stand, take aim and fire. They'd fix their ends to the chimneys and solid walls around them as the hooks looped over the top of the craft, then stand back and wait for the slack to be taken up. Then, with a high-pitched twang

Cass could only feel, the cables would pull taut, knocking the car off its plane and dragging it down into their web. Once it was on the ground there was no escape.

Quarters and the others weren't the only ones to wander this far off-Grid. They had to be fast to make sure they got what they needed before the competition came. Some they could discourage. Others though, especially the hunter gangs, were far too dangerous to argue with. It was best for everyone if they avoided any confrontations.

Focus. It comes.

She opened her eyes and stared at the chimney in front of her. It would do. There were deep cable gouges in its cement already, but it could take a few more. Just get the shot right.

Cass slowly stood up and peered over the lip. There it was. Headlights weaving back and forth in the murk, obviously lost. Flying lower than usual in order to find some sort of landmark to navigate by. All the better.

She whistled and the others stood as one. Everything was ready. They wouldn't miss.

Just then Cass felt a strange twinge in the back of her neck. Something about the car was wrong. Its movement, its feel, its sound, perhaps. She glanced across the rooftops and saw Quarters aiming his bow. He obviously didn't hear anything. She put her bow to her shoulder and forced the growing tightness back down into her belly. Ignore all distractions. Don't fuck this up.

The car was over them then; the fuzziness emanating from inside it, washing over her. She felt rather than saw the hooks release and fly over the craft. Five cables, all on target, their glowing lines shining like thin fingers pulling into a fist around their prey. Just as they began to squeeze, however, the car jerked abruptly to the right and dipped away, down into the buildings.

Cass sucked in her breath. No way the driver could have seen them and reacted like that. And no autopilot programme took that kind of risk. She watched the car try to right itself again and slide sideways, clipping its tail on the roof of another broken-down, deserted house. The fucker's going to crash anyway. Still, they could have done without the extra noise.

She looked across at Quarters, who shrugged his shoulders elaborately and flashed a grin at her. The next moment he was sliding down the gutter to the street below. Why question good fortune? Just react. Even if it crashed, they'd manage to salvage something.

Cass dropped the bow and slid down the tiled rooftop on her back. As her heels clipped the gutter she twisted and flipped in midair, turning her body to the wall and grabbing the pipe with one hand. Then it was just a straight slide down the three storeys to the street below.

Already she was faster than the others. She crouched down and waited for them to move in front as she'd been instructed. Her reflexes were sharper than theirs now. She was quicker, more agile, but she was still a newbie. She had to wait her turn.

As she waited for the signal she tried to grasp what it was she'd felt as the car had approached. Something had been off, yet familiar. Something that didn't belong here. The puddles of water at her feet flashed back her reflection and she almost glimpsed it, another face through the water, reaching out to her.

She felt the pull in her gut and started to run. Forget it. It was time to feed.

Her heels rang down the alley, bouncing off the sheer walls surrounding her. Cass could feel the hum, the disturbance in the air. She couldn't hear it as such, but it was there to be read all the same.

She reached her senses out to the surrounding area. There was nothing yet, but it was only a matter of time. This far off-Grid stayed pretty empty most of the time, but those who wandered these lanes were best avoided altogether. They needed to get in and out of the crash site quickly, strip the car of what they needed and go before there were any ugly confrontations.

Cass could handle herself, they all could. As long as they didn't run into any professionals.

The others had already reached the car, she could feel their eagerness, almost smell it. She rounded the corner and stopped as the flames from the crash lit up the wall in front of her.

Deep breath.

Cass closed her eyes and forced her breathing back down. She sent her senses shooting out around them, searching for trouble. The night was stretched out around her like a calm pool of water, no disturbances, no ripples in the skin. Just the crash site itself and…

Cass focused harder as the wave washed across her. There was something.

She tried to pin it down and found herself turning on the spot. Towards the flames, towards the heat and steam. She opened her eyes and stared straight down the lane at the burning wreck. That was it. Something off, the same familiar dread she'd felt when the car had approached them. Part fear, part something else. Danger.

She trotted down the middle of the road towards the site, more carefully now, following the path the others had taken. The feeling was definitely getting stronger. Part of her wanted to sprint after them, after him, make sure he was okay, but the wiser animal side of her protested. Go slow. Know your enemy.

Her belly tightened as she got closer to the corner. She gritted her teeth and forced her feet, which no longer wanted to move, further forwards. Five more steps and she was around it.

The road opened into a large square, in the middle of which was the wreckage of the car. Orange flames were still licking across it, but most of the fuel seemed to have burnt off already. It didn't look dangerous. Pieces of metal from the craft and rubble from the buildings were strewn behind it where it had skidded down on its belly. Where was Quarters?

He was there somewhere, she could feel him, though only faintly.

A dark shadow flitted across the wreckage and Cass automatically crouched down. What was that? She crept forwards on her haunches, keeping an eye on the burning light of the wreck.

There it was again. Hunched over, rocking back and forth, as if searching for something. Then it stopped and raised its head. It was Quarters.

Cass began to stand but suddenly froze in place. Her legs wouldn't let her be seen. There was something very wrong here. It was Quarters, but not him. His eyes were blank, completely empty and lifeless. Glazed over and alien. She sank back down into the shadows and watched.

Where could the others be? There was no sign of them at all, just Quarters and emptiness and...

Cass sank even lower as the light from the flames threw up another shadow, off to the side of the wreck. A single figure, standing tall and very still. A woman. She was watching Quarters too.

He was on all fours now, crawling back and forth in place, faster than before, almost panicked. Finally, he turned towards the other figure and crawled directly towards her.

Cass wanted to cry out, to reach out and stop him, but couldn't. The feeling in the pit of her stomach was all consuming now, rushing up her spine and over her mind, stopping all action. All she could do was watch as the figure opened its arms and Quarters disappeared into them.

Then it was gone, all of it. Like somebody had flipped a switch, the feeling emptied out of her and she found herself on her feet, facing the empty, burning wreckage. Quarters was gone. The figure was gone. Everyone was gone.

***

"We've had frequent complaints about you from both your fellow officers and the clients we serve, Poe, as I'm sure you know. Subtlety is not your strong point."

That morning, in the captain's office, Detective Poe was receiving his new assignment. "I merely endeavour to uncover the simple…"

"Yes, yes, Poe. Uncover the simple truths behind the act to better illuminate the crime. That's the point man, not all truths are simple, in fact most aren't. They're always wrapped up in consequence. I'm more concerned, however, with the complaints from within the force."

"They disapprove of my methods."

"You're damn right they do. Disapprove of being constantly made fun of as well. Why do you feel the need to intimidate them with your little notepad? Surely the standard recorders are just as effective. More so."

"Captain, as I've mentioned to you in the past the very act of forming my observations into words allows me to clarify and arrange my ideas. I find things easier to compute."

"And that's exactly what you are, Poe, a computer, a fact you should never allow to stray too far from your mind. Computers process data and come back with the answer expected of them. They do not have sudden flashes of intuition. This is what makes the other detectives nervous. How you do it is beyond me, and frankly I don't care. Just know that there will come a time when others do care. People do not trust what they do not understand. They may suffer it while it serves their purpose, but once it ceases to do so they will turn on it with something very close to glee. There should not be a ghost in the machine."

Poe grinned to himself now at the memory. Ghost in the machine. He liked it.

Back in the present, Detective Poe stood off to one side of the smouldering crash site and silently doodled in his notepad. The other detectives were scanning the area, tablets in their hands plugged into the ports behind their ears, soaking up sense data from their assigned six-by-six squares of the crash grid. Poe preferred his notepad. It helped him think, and it annoyed the other detectives, which was always a bonus.

Well now, we should make the most of things while we can then, shouldn't we?

He flipped his notepad closed and strode over to the flaming wreck. Steam from the constant rain was curling around the feet of the nearest other detective. Gantry was his name. Useless fellow. "Hullo there, Gantry! Any luck?"

Gantry's eyes flicked up from where they had been scouring the ground and formed themselves into a set of displeasure. "Poe."

He acknowledged him with a nod and tried to get back to his work.

"Any discoveries?"

The fact was that apart from his notepad the one thing that helped Poe get his thoughts in order was bothering other people. Especially other detectives. They were easy targets.

Gantry raised his head again. "Nothing to report so far. Why don't you access the Grid and download the full report yourself? You'll sense everything I am."

"Including me?"

Poe grinned insolently into his face.

"It is doubtful your presence is an important factor for this crime scene, Poe, so no. Now if you will excuse me I…"

"Ah, but how do we know that, Gantry? Who makes this decision as to what is and is not important information? For all we know I'm the most important part of this crime scene, we just don't see it yet."

Gantry didn't bother with a reply, just wandered off to another section of ground and started scanning.

"What did I tell you, Adlai? Useless to a man." Poe whispered to his ever-present intellectual companion. "May as well be working with a bunch of robots."

***

Adlai had always considered himself too lucky to be religious. His parents had tried, Catholic schools from ages five to eighteen, church on Sundays from birth. But when there's nothing to ask God for but a new bike, what is the point?

His father had noticed Adlai's fading interest and tried to revive it by taking him along to a different church. Charismatics. Lots of people dancing around singing in tongues, having visions, being touched by the Spirit. All very exciting for an impressionable twelve-year-old, you would have thought.

Unfortunately, all Adlai saw were ugly, handicapped and poor people. It made him realise consciously what had been running around in the back of his mind for some time now. Religion was for those less fortunate than him. Like government care. It would be greedy of him to try to take a share when he so clearly didn't need it.

Yes, government care was a good comparison. He could do without it, so he should. In fact, to stretch the point a little further, he should start investing in his own religion. Private health cover if you will.

So he started skipping Sunday mass, disappearing instead to the park with a good book. Happily shivering away in the cold, squinting in the fading light of the afternoon, immersed in other worlds. He made the decision to give up on organised religion altogether.

Of course, he didn't tell his parents that. His mother had started out with such high hopes for her son. Born near the start of a new millennium, the whole world open to him. Religion was a duty; it was part of life. You just did it, no questions asked.

The household itself wasn't particularly devout. They were as secular as the next modern family when it came to entertainment, no censorship came into play. Adlai was free to read, watch and do what he wanted, within reason, and like all teenagers he soon discovered that what his parents didn't know couldn't hurt them. And when it came to the modern plaything of choice, the computer, his parents didn't know very much at all.

Books were all well and good, but when it came to religious experiences something that engaged all of your senses, not just your imagination, had a distinct advantage. Handheld consoles replaced his book in the park each Sunday. By the time he hit sixteen and virtual reality finally became a real possibility, there was no going back.

Back then you couldn't just jack in to the nearest port and go. You needed a powerful computer to run the latest software, nothing portable, and ports were right at the bleeding edge. Adlai finally had to bite the bullet and face up to his parents about his Sunday activities. He was sixteen and could make his own decisions, there would be no more sneaking off to the park. They'd tried their best, raised him well, but a large part of good parenting is knowing when to let your children go, and it was time to let go of the reins and give him his head.

They didn't buy a word of it, but Adlai didn't care, so long as they bought the computer. Every Sunday when his mother went to church to pray for his ungrateful soul, Adlai wandered up to his room and plugged himself in to a different kind of religion.

After all, who needed God when you had VR?

****

Cass was huddled down in the cold of an abandoned third-storey storeroom, watching the last embers of the fire blink out. She'd skipped out of the crash site as soon as Quarters had disappeared. That strange feeling had left, only to be replaced by another, more familiar one. Cops were on their way.

The car must have had an important passenger for the cops to bother coming this far off-Grid at all, let alone so quickly. Maybe there was something valuable in the mess of the wreckage, maybe she should have had a better look. She hadn't been thinking particularly clearly at the time.

She remembered Quarters's face in the flickering firelight and shivered. No, she'd left at just the right time. Cass shivered and hunched her shoulders together, squeezing her eyes shut to block out the memories.

When she'd first wandered off-Grid, who knows how long ago it was now, it had been a night just like this. It was always wet and cold, but this emptiness, this loneliness was exactly how she remembered. She'd been thrilled at first to have made it at all. There was no point where she'd reached a boundary and crossed it, she'd just followed the directions, kept travelling along the River and eventually noticed the constant neon glow of the Grid had faded, the clatter and noise from the corporate attractions and their patrons sank away. She looked around and saw dark streets leading away in every direction. It began to rain.

The Grid was miles behind her, impossibly distant and out of reach. Even if she'd wanted to, she couldn't re-enter it. Now it was a mere glow on the horizon, getting further away with every step you took towards it. There was no way back.

There had to have been a transition point, a border between life on and off-Grid, but if so, she'd missed it. Like every other major decision in life, she'd taken it without realising it. It was the best way to be. This way she only had to worry about the consequences.

The rain felt good. Cool on her shoulders, real. She could feel herself becoming more alert, more awake, more alive.

There was something coming.

Instinct made her step into a darkened doorway. It was probably nothing, but she knew she had to trust her first choice. She'd heard the stories of what could happen to you out here. Best to watch and wait for now.

Her spine tensed as the figure came closer. She suddenly felt very exposed in the doorway and squeezed further back into the shadows. It was only when she began to feel dizzy that she realised she was holding her breath.

As the figure walked past the doorway, she let it out and smiled. It was only a kid.

Barely ten years old, scruffily dressed but smiling. Shaggy blonde hair and a mischievous grin fixed to his face. Cass felt an immediate fellowship as his eyes passed over her hiding place. This was lucky. Her first contact might explain some things. She leant forward to step out into the street.

A thin, strong arm wrapped around her torso, holding her in place, its hand clamped down over her mouth. She tensed to fight as a hot breath whispered into her ear. "Be silent. Quiet as a mouse."

A male voice. Cass could feel the words, feel them through the tips of his fingers, through the pressure of his chest on her back. She didn't need to hear them. His arms were warm around her. She waited.

The figure in the street turned towards their doorway and raised its head, sniffing the wind. It peered directly at them, and for the first time Cass noticed the strange glint in its eyes. It was unnatural, steely, hungry. She held her breath and felt the hand around her mouth drop away.

The boy in the street sniffed again, sensing something. His lips curled back to reveal sharpened teeth. Then another noise off to the side caused him to spin away. A muffled oath and the slap of footsteps running away. The figure in the street – more animal than boy now – crouched down and sprang into the alley, scuttling after the retreating footsteps. Cass noticed her tension dripping away as it left.

The arm was still wrapped around her, no longer holding her in place but lingering nonetheless. "A feeder, hunting for new blood. Almost got some too. Don't worry, Simps'll get rid of it."

Cass stepped forward slowly and turned, letting the arm drop away. It followed her out of the shadows, leading its owner, a thin, dark-haired man. Man or boy? She couldn't tell. He grinned back at her and raised his hand again, this time to clasp hers in a handshake. "Hi. I'm Quarters. I just saved your life."

Cass felt the grin on her face and snapped her eyes open. Her arms were wrapped around her legs, remembering the warmth that had seeped away now. Taken away just like Quarters had been.

It wasn't just that he'd disappeared either, she could sense his absence completely. He was gone, wiped out of existence. He hadn't just been taken somewhere; he'd been entirely removed.

Like the body of whoever had been driving that car.

***

The air was wet and dirty as Poe strode down the lane. He liked the feel of the rain on his face. It woke him up. It felt real. "All of this, Adlai, all these ruins, this poverty and emptiness, it's all real. It's exciting, don't you think? I haven't felt this way since I was your age, just a young graduate. Since the last time I was out here actually."

"Have you been assigned out here before, sir?"

"Oh yes, every now and then there's real work to be done, real investigations to be had. Real problems to solve. It all happens off-Grid. Those robots we left earlier are no good out here. Can't think for themselves you see. No natural ability."

Poe tried to soak all the sensations in. He had to begin to understand the area again. "This is what real detective work is, my young man. Get into the role. Understand the environment to the point that you notice the small imperfections, the differences that point you in the right direction. Then you pick up the clues."

He placed his hands behind his back and strolled casually down the centre of the road. No danger of cars out here. The victim's must have been the first in years. The victim. Kane Sanderson. Musician. Well off, single, no known complications in his life. What the hell was he doing off-Grid?

If he had certain tastes which couldn't be serviced privately at home – though those were getting few and far between these days – he could still have found something closer in. Money wasn't a problem. Besides, that wouldn't explain the crash. No, that wasn't the way to be thinking.

The question is not why, it is where. Where was he going?

Poe stopped in the middle of the street. "You know, Adlai, I think we need to spend some real time out here. If I can trust my instincts, and I think that I can, then this is one of those cases where we need to let the clues come to us. We need to throw caution to the wind as it were, jump in the deep end, all that stuff."

"Get into some trouble, sir?"

"Quite right, Adlai! Quite right. But first I suppose I should follow the correct procedures. You don't mind, of course, it's just that the captain frowns on me bringing others in with me when I make my reports."

Poe reached into his coat and brought out a small plug which he inserted into the port just behind his ear.

Immediately, he found himself in a small waiting room outside a large oak door. It was bare except for a lone, uncomfortable-looking chair and a small desk complete with a secretary. She was a bit too attractive to be real.

"The captain will see you in just a moment."

She spoke the words without looking up from the ancient typewriter she was clattering away on. Why the captain felt the need to indulge in such a dated answering machine was beyond him.

Just then the large doors swung open and the secretary spoke again. "The captain will see you now."

He almost said thanks, but remembered he was talking to a machine. A machine with great calves, but a machine, nonetheless. He enjoyed the view as he wandered past her into the dark of the captain's office. Maybe he did have a point.

"That's enough of that, Poe."

The gruff voice reached out and pulled him into the room. Poe found himself standing straighter, a reaction which always annoyed him but one he could do little about.

The captain was, as always, sitting behind an enormous slab of oak, completely bare except for a single electric lamp with a dark green shade. It gave off almost no light, but then it probably wasn't meant to. It was there to create menacing shadows.

"You need to learn to watch those thoughts of yours, son, especially when you've invited someone in to share them with you."

The captain motioned to the lone chair opposite, but Poe shook his head and continued to stand. It always made him uncomfortable to be sitting in VR while his body was standing out there. Made him feel slightly queasy.

"Anything to report?"

"Nothing so far, Captain, that's why I'm here. I'd like to request some extended time off-Grid."

That brought a reaction, if only a slight shift of weight as the captain leaned forward. "Any particular reason?"

"I think it would help with the case, sir. Basically, I think we're looking at this the wrong way. We need to find the wheres and whys, the motive behind the events. Besides, there are enough other detectives around to do the drudge work."

The captain rewarded this with a long stare. "You know something, Poe? You think entirely too much to still be a detective. I'm sure I've mentioned this before."

Poe kept his mind blank and waited. No use getting into trouble.

"Approved. But I want full and regular reports, from you alone, you understand? The less I know about your peculiar habits the better. Dismissed."

The captain dropped his head back down and Poe turned to leave. "And Poe? Leave my secretary alone on the way out, will you?"

Poe pulled himself back into reality and pocketed the plug. He took a deep breath and looked around. He was at an intersection, all four streets looked exactly the same. One was as good as any other.

"Come along, Adlai, let's see what kind of trouble we can get into."

***

Adlai was in trouble. He ducked back down behind the thick concrete pylon as the bullets zipped by overhead. They were still coming. He'd been stuck here for hours now, trying to fight his way back to the lines, back to his group, but he wasn't making any headway.

He poked his eyes back around the corner and waited for the dust to settle. There. A slight movement, not thirty metres from where he lay. A black metal helmet bobbing in the dirt.

He slid his rifle out from underneath his body and took aim. There was no use waiting anymore, his team had obviously given him up for dead. May as well cause some trouble while he still could.

He took aim and concentrated on the sights. The crosshairs slid across the target as his muscles tensed. Concentrate on your breathing. Let your finger squeeze the trigger.

The helmet disintegrated in a shower of red and black pieces as the bullet ripped through it. Adlai smiled to himself, then sprang to his feet and ran, leaving the rifle where it lay. It couldn't help him now.

Angry cries flew out from the trenches behind him as he ran. They must be able to see him by now, he wasn't that quick, not yet. Moments later the first shots thudded into the dirt around him as he skipped through the rubble. Not that fast, but fast enough.

His gang had driven into the territory in a rough wedge, then fallen apart as they were surrounded and scattered. They'd become overconfident again, pushed too far, always trying to dance along that edge, where the real thrills lay. They were all still too young to know better.

Another bullet cracked into the concrete beside his head as he zipped past another broken building. They were getting closer, probably trying to drive him into some sort of trap. He had to be smarter than they were. Smarter and faster.

He concentrated his will and focused. There was a six-foot-high wall ahead of him, coming closer every step. He could do this.

More cries sounded behind him. This was the one chance left. Time seemed to slow as he approached the wall, his senses taking everything in. Three more steps, then a leap, simple as that. He could picture what was going to happen. He was there.

The bullet blew through his knee and crippled him in an instant, his forward momentum bringing him sliding through the dirt to tumble to rest against the base of the wall. It would have been funny if it wasn't so painful. He raised his head up and could just make out the figures striding towards him through the dust. A gun pointing towards him, then the fire of the port burning him back into reality.

Back in the bar, Adlai reached behind his ear and scratched the scar where his data port used to be. It often tingled when he thought about it. They'd been a big step at the time, at least for some. The kids had embraced it, the removal of another obstacle between themselves and the ultimate VR experience. Soon it became unusual not to have one.

The older generation, like his parents, had declined. He suspected they still saw VR as a circus, an amusing sideshow, definitely not worth cracking your head open for. He'd tried convincing them that age was no longer an excuse, that they could be whatever age they wanted to be in the expanding universes inside the ports, what they came to name the River, but they no longer wanted to change. They'd stepped out of time.

They died together and he imagined they were happier for it. He spent his mourning period lost in other people's multiplying realities.

Multiply they did. He wasn't the only misfit to find the possibilities of VR intriguing. As it grew, as more designers and tinkers came on board, each pulling in a different direction, the outside world began to take control. It had happened with every other medium in human history, the River was no different. Endless possibilities were far too dangerous to be left in the hands of just anyone. Better they were centrally controlled. That was where the Grid began.

The River relied on hardware, so those who owned the hardware banded together to take control. The Grid became the main gathering place, more and more power sucking into it, dimming other areas in comparison. The casual user never stepped outside of its boundaries. Pretty soon for most people it *was* VR. Every port led into it.

For Adlai and the other hardcore users, the Grid was anathema, the exact opposite of what VR was supposed to be all about. They found themselves pushed out into the dark corners of the River, scrambling for power and space, fighting among themselves, games turning into real battles for supremacy. The golden age was over.

Adlai took a drink and stared at the line of bottles behind the bar. They're a corporation too. You don't seem to mind being under their control.

He gripped his glass tighter but took another drink just the same.

So he wasn't as principled as he once was, so what? It's called growing up. You get more jaded and accepting until one day you look around and realise you're an adult and it's too late to pull yourself out. He couldn't be bothered getting angry anymore.

What was the problem anyway? So the powers are distant and faceless – remind you of anyone? Who was it that said you could never take a picture of God?

The worshippers didn't seem to mind. The Grid grew and grew until you had... until you had this.

Adlai looked out the window at the darkness and the greasy rain. A pale glow hovered on the horizon. The Grid. Sucking energy into it, leaving the rest of the universe of the River in cold darkness. It was self-perpetuating. The uglier the real world got, the more time you spent online escaping it, which led to the real world just getting uglier.

He rubbed his scar again. He'd cut that umbilical cord. Spirituality, escape wasn't controlled by anyone else but him, not anymore. God was no longer in a cage.

Now he was in a bottle.

***

Dark shadows lurked on both sides of the street as Poe wandered further off-Grid. He walked down the centre of the lane, head down, hands thrust into pockets, eyes narrowed into slits, lost in his own world. After a while, he began to whistle.

Nothing conscious, just a simple tune that was stuck in his head. A few notes, round and round, never reaching an obvious end. Stretching themselves one into the other.

A loud clatter to his left stopped him, and he turned in time to see an old metal garbage can roll across the gutter. "Looks like we may have some company. Don't let it bother you now, Adlai. Whoever it is, if they particularly want to see me, they'll get out here eventually. Just keep the old eyes open."

Poe liked to encourage a passive outlook on life, particularly when it came to his own safety. It made things more interesting.

Fifty metres further on he heard a light foot skip across the road behind him but fought the urge to turn around. Not long now. "Have I told you before about the natives out here, Adlai? Unpleasant folk, most of them. Dangerous. Have to keep your eyes open and your hand close to your wallet. Not to mention your gun. Still, let's see if we can't tempt this one out with a little bait?"

He swung his coat out and over his hip, revealing a heavy looking pouch hanging from his belt. "This one's no real threat, otherwise we would have been hit by now. My guess is a pickpocket, a street urchin. Gets by on what he can steal. Don't let appearances fool you, though, my boy, some of them can be particularly nasty."

There was a whisper of movement and Poe spun sharply to his left and grabbed a young wrist just before it cut the belt on his hip. At the same time, he stepped out and away from the other arm and caught it as it swung in a wide, lazy hook.

Sure enough, a kid. "Well, hello there, my boy. Looking for something?"

Poe squeezed the thin wrist and a clatter told him the blade in the boy's hand was no longer a danger. He pulled the would-be pickpocket closer to get a good look at his face. He was young, probably only ten or so, underneath what looked like fifteen years of dirt.

The boy struggled but got nowhere. Poe held on patiently and waited for him to tire. If there was one thing he'd learnt in his years on the force, it was that nothing occurred by accident. Everything led to an answer, you just had to be open enough to see it.

"Lemme go!"

"Ah, he speaks!"

He looked down at the road and saw the curved blade the boy had swung gleaming back at him. One of those River Blades, as they'd come to be known. Nasty things. A quick kick and the evil looking weapon bounced off into the darkness of the nearest alleyway. "Now, what would a young man like yourself be doing with a thing like that? Trying to cut my belt, obviously. Hopefully not trying to cut anything else."

The boy had been straining for the blade, but now that it was gone the madness seemed to leave him and he stopped struggling. The blade hadn't had a hold of him completely. He must have only found it recently for its effect to pass so quickly.

"Please, sir, I just need money for my father. He's sick, sir. I'm sorry, sir."

"Enough with the 'sirs'. Sick you say? What's the matter with him?"

"We don't know, sir, I mean, he just lies there, like he's asleep."

Poe let his wrists go and the boy sprang back and away. Three steps further and he was pulled off his feet, ending up on the ground, staring up at the sky, wondering what had just happened. The thin wire lasso wrapped around one wrist glinted in the streetlights. "Incredibly useful things those cuffs. Police issue, don't you know. You won't be able to get too far unless I run out the line a little."

He pulled back his coat to reveal the source of the line in a small spool on his hip. "Besides, I thought you wanted me to help someone?"

Seeing he was stuck, the young pickpocket relaxed again. "Yes, sir, my uncle."

"Your uncle now, is it? Regular epidemic running through your family isn't there?"

It was obvious the kid was lying, but there was something behind it. Probably just wanted to lure him off into the dark somewhere, into some sort of trap, somewhere he and his friends could clean him out and disappear. No, certainly wouldn't be a good idea to go with him. "Still, when did good ideas get you anywhere, hmm?"

"Sir?"

"Come on, son, get up. I need you to lead the way."

The boy's eyes positively lit up and he sprang to his feet. Probably couldn't believe his luck. He'd have to work on his poker face if he was going to last long out here. Not all his victims would be so cavalier.

***

She'd watched the cops scan the area, pacing back and forth, sucking up every last bit of sense data. Cops never did get it. You couldn't trust facts out here. This was the jungle, you had to rely on instinct. It told her the body of the driver was gone, long before they cleaned up the wreck and discovered it for themselves.

Cass turned away and stared off into the distance at the dull glow that was the Grid, reaching out to her through the rain, promising warmth and safety and a sterile life. There was no way back there now. Maybe that's where both the driver and Quarters had ended up. Returned to the first level, having to fight their way up and out. She knew that wasn't true. They were gone.

There was nothing for it but to head deeper off-Grid. She had some skills, she could survive on her own, at least for a while.

The drumming hum of the rain lulled her senses as she wandered. It felt right to lose herself, feel her consciousness spread out like the surface of a lake. Tense, clean, waiting for the first ripple.

And there it was. She could feel it at the base of her spine. Not hear it, but feel the sound, the presence. The threat. That didn't take long.

The hunters were out. They must have noticed the commotion, maybe even contacted the cops themselves, they were known to have links where they shouldn't. Someone had noticed her and they'd been sent out to get rid of any witnesses. She was prey now, fresh meat.

Meat. That was how she felt, her body strange and unfamiliar, like something had been released when Quarters had disappeared into that figure's arms. There was an electricity running through her veins. She looked the same, dressed the same, but she was alive. More alive than ever.

Cass felt a clattering reach across the air towards her as one of the hunters stumbled in an alley next to hers. She would have to move quickly if she was to escape. Above her was a dark opening where a window used to be, only six feet in the air. She sprang up into it, not bothering to use her hands, and paused in the shadows.

From her vantage point she could see a lone hunter wander around the corner and start down the alley. There was a dangerous edge around him, an absolute hunger. His fangs flashed. Cass shrank back further into the shadows though she knew he couldn't see her. Wait for him to walk through then skip out behind him and away. There was no reasoning with this animal.

She closed her eyes and concentrated on her breathing. Slow it down. Calm. Quiet as a mouse.

Her foot nudged something, and her eyes snapped open to search the shadows at her feet. There it was. The curved blade at her feet seemed to reach out to her hand as she bent down to wrap her fingers around it.

As she brought it up to her face the dim light from the street flitted across its edge and stopped the breath in her lungs. It was beautiful. It gleamed with power and threat and something more. Cool efficiency. The hunter himself faded into the background behind its glow. And suddenly she knew there would be no running away.

The hunter paused halfway down the alley. She could sense his indecisiveness, his frustration. He was about to turn and leave. Cass looked down at her feet again, she somehow knew to, and saw a glass shard lying near her boot. She slid it off the edge of the sill with her toe.

The shatter made the hunter tense immediately and stride towards the sound. The desperation, the hunger had overcome his doubt and fear. Cass found herself smiling as he approached.

When he was standing directly beneath her, she felt a moment of hesitation, baulking at what she was about to do. She knew it was the last time she'd ever feel guilt or doubt again.

Cass sprang down onto his shoulders, feet first, crumpling him to the ground. She curved backwards towards his prone legs and sliced the blade as deep as she could, quickly, across the tendons on the back of his knees.

She felt a shudder pass through his body, but no sound. The pain hadn't had a chance to register, and it wouldn't.

In one movement she kicked down the arm that was reaching up at her, pinning it to the street, and sliced the blade up his side, across the shoulders and deep into the side of his neck. It only took a moment for his body to relax into death.

And then it was done. She stood and leapt back into the shadows of her hiding spot, out through the dark, ruined building, across the rooftops and away.

It wasn't until she was streets away that she realised she was smiling.

***

Adlai had never understood faith. His parents had it, the priest he used to spend Sundays ignoring had it, the other parishioners seemed to have it, even his friends, who acted just as bored and put upon as he did, even they seemed to have it. They all believed without question.

He used to put it down to the fact that he was much smarter than everyone else. He was right, they were wrong, simple as that. Age had erased that foothold. There's only so long you can go on ignoring the achievements of others without facing the facts. He wasn't special, or different, or better. He was average, just like everyone else. So why couldn't he believe?

He was sure if he concentrated hard enough, he could pull it off. Convince himself. Trouble was he couldn't even bring himself to pretend. What was the point? What comfort did these people get from believing in something so far from being proven, so unworldly? Where was their curiosity?

It didn't matter which religion you were talking about, whether you spent time in synagogues, mosques or churches, the central idea of faith seemed to be the same. Belief without the possibility of proof. What was he missing that everyone else had, this need to have something to believe in?

As he got older and circumstances changed, it never made any more sense. As the VR universes squirmed into people's daily routines, he watched just another example of it. People spent hours, days at a time in worlds not of their creation, convincing themselves of its reality. Sure, the hardware, the improved graphics and speed made it an easier pill to swallow, but when you got down to it people believed because they wanted to. They needed to. VR worked because everyone wanted to believe. It was easier to believe.

They used to tell stories of the suffering of the saints, gruesome, bloody tales of death and torture suffered as a consequence of not renouncing faith. They were just the thing to keep eleven-year-old boys interested in church. But to Adlai, faith was the easy part. Once you had an answer, it was much harder to question it and leave yourself staring at the abyss than simply believing and having your hand held.

The viral growth of VR wasn't surprising for exactly this reason. Convincing yourself there's a higher power judging, watching and looking after you was no different from believing in the realities you slotted yourself into day after day. They used to call it a revolution, but not Adlai. Forsaking one reality, one set of fictions for another was no surprise. It was entrenched in human nature.

Adlai needed more than just the opportunity to believe. He needed help to silence that annoying little voice that kept popping up and asking questions, the one that kept snapping him back from happiness. There had been different incarnations over the years, but he'd found one now that looked like it could be with him for the long haul.

He took another drink.

***

Poe let the boy lead and slipped his hand inside his coat to rest on the hilt of his gun. He didn't want to have to use it, but then he didn't want to end up dead in a gutter either.

There were worse things out here than pickpockets.

The first thing Poe noticed was the smell. It lay heavy over the entire building, soaking into the wood, curling through the shattered windows and crawling into every crack in the walls. Something was definitely not right about this place. As for the sort of person who chose to live in it…

He let the young pickpocket lead him further inside the dark doorway but then halted to allow time for his eyes to adjust to the gloom. It was far darker than out on the street, as if whatever was causing that stench had decided to alter the natural light for added effect. Poe was getting more and more interested with every step.

It had been his experience that most crimes of the modern age were best solved by diving in headfirst and waiting to see where the current dragged you. If not solved, the crimes would perhaps at least be understood. Crime wasn't simple these days, or rather, it had become so simple as to dumbfound all but the most brilliant or naïve. Poe was proud to consider himself both.

In a world where most people spent increasing amounts of time plugged in to another reality, material goods and therefore material wants faded. So too did material crime. What was the point of stealing anything when you could just plug yourself in and find the right corner of the Grid? As a result, criminals tended to be far less simple and predictable. Where once you were almost guaranteed to get your man simply by following procedure, a more creative approach had become necessary.

Over the years Poe had come to trust his instincts, especially the more eccentric ones. He was proud of his achievement. Eccentricity was underrated.

Poe reached out through the ink and touched the boy's shoulder. Onward.

The building itself was a complete mess. Even in the darkness he could make out the partial walls, sagging frames and streams of rainwater washing down from higher floors. There had to be better options around. It's not like there was a shortage of abandoned buildings out here to choose from.

And the smell. It was getting stronger as they wandered further in. A rotting sweetness, it gave Poe a disturbingly familiar twinge. He knew what that smell signified. Death.

The pickpocket had evidently come to the same conclusion as round the next corner Poe felt the cuff wire tighten momentarily before snapping back at him. He heard the young boy scuttle away and let him go. Must have had another blade on him or hidden one here. Still, he'd led him this far.

There was an orange glow further up the corridor, and Poe continued towards it. He was only mildly surprised when he noticed his gun was in his hand. "Breathe in softly, son, it's only a smell. No need to imagine what could be the cause. No need for gag reflexes. Just air, just molecules sucking down your throat, into your lungs and out again."

Finally, he rounded a corner that opened into what used to be a kitchen of some sort. The room was lit by a fire in an old oil drum, surrounded by piles of trash. Scraps of food and wrappers were littered everywhere, and in the far corner was the reason everything smelt so bad. A drawn figure of a man, completely emaciated, slumped across an old army surplus cot. He looked like he'd been dead for weeks.

Poe wondered when the kid had been here last, and whether he'd ever come back. He hoped the dead man wasn't actually his father.

The smell was lessened by the fire – who'd been feeding it? – and the earlier sense of dread was gone now that the cause was here in front of him. He walked forward to get a closer look, but a yard from the body he suddenly stopped. "Now what do you make of that, young Adlai?"

He leaned forwards to get a closer look at the man's face without blocking out the light of the fire. Something was off. "There."

A flicker of movement, underneath the eyelids. He stared again, trying to soak in as much information as he could before his brain attacked it. There it was again, his eyes were definitely moving underneath their lids, snapping back and forth.

"This man, my young friend, is asleep."

***

Cass woke to the sound of applause and rolled over. It was just the rain hammering down outside her window, so hard you could feel it in your fingertips. Her brain was still foggy from sleep, lost in forgotten universes and selves. She lay still in bed and stared at the rain as her mind sorted itself out.

She felt wretched, guilty almost. She wasn't hungover, there was no one else in the room, so it wasn't the obvious. What was it then? This dread that seeped through her, making her toss and turn in the dark and wake up feeling strained and more tired than when she went to bed.

It was Monday, that had to be it. Monday meant work, meant a whole week of work in fact, drudgery stretching out in front of you. Every Monday was the same. Tuesdays weren't much better, in fact it wasn't really until Thursday that she slept the whole night through, untroubled by dark dreams. They'd been getting darker too, at least, so she thought. She could no longer remember them.

That hadn't always been the way. She'd had very vivid dreams when younger, she used to wake up and roll over to the side of the bed, reach under it to the pad of paper stored for just such an occasion and scribble down every last detail. Often it flowed over more than one page. These days she neither wrote nor remembered. Nothing more than images and flashes, fleeting and dark. Rain. Monsters. Blood.

It had been that way ever since the accident. Dreams were no longer a place to escape to. She didn't want to see what they brought up from the depths.

Maybe it was just that she hated her job. Everyone hated their jobs though, at least, everyone she knew. Jobs were dull. They seemed to have got duller over the years, or maybe she just knew more now. Someone at work had told her they thought it was all part of the scam to make you spend more time plugged in. They made the real world so unattractive that you just had to tune in and drop out.

Cass wasn't that paranoid. But the dreams, the way they flashed in and out now, that had something to do with VR. It was too vivid and strong now, too bright and shiny, pushing everything else back out of your brain, leaving it a polished surface with nowhere for dreams to cling on to. That was why she tried to leave it alone. Turned off the field before crawling into bed and lay staring, wishing real dreams back into her, no matter how dark.

It didn't work. Maybe it was part of "their" plan, whoever they were. Make you miss the dreams, the time spent plugged in. Bring you to a point where you couldn't stand to spend a day without at least a short visit. She looked around the office each day at the glazed eyes and knew that for most people it worked. They couldn't resist it.

It wasn't good for you; Cass was convinced of that. She'd enjoyed it, had her fun, but knew when something wasn't right. VR felt wrong. Your dreams multiplied on top of each other, and the sick separation, the tear when it all ended. It was too much.

Cass turned her head and watched the raindrops slide down the window. Life should be lived on this side, in reality, no matter how dull and grey it made itself out to be. The drops streaked together and pooled at the base of the glass, warping the image outside.

No matter how lonely.

***

Adlai sat very still, watching the prone body in front of him. They'd captured him days earlier, another spy for the Grid. They were coming in regularly now, small time users who wanted a shortcut to the top, coders who came in too late, young hot shots who wanted the power to twist the world around them to their liking, but found all the tools locked away, the usual tricks already sealed off. There were two choices, either start at the bottom with everyone else, or slink over to the Grid and offer your services. They always accepted.

Adlai could understand, he knew the frustration of being just like everyone else. At least, he used to know. Now he was one of the few they sent saps like this after.

They'd caught him far too easily really. Another raid on one of their war scenes, trying to hit them while they were distracted with their games. It never worked. The powers behind the Grid didn't care, there were plenty more where this boy came from.

He wondered if this one at least had a chance to experience something of what he was helping to destroy. The freedom that the River could offer, the possibilities, the pure pleasure of losing yourself in someone else's fantasy. More than pleasure, illusion was a necessity, you had to escape reality in order to survive this life. VR was a place to do that, a place to chase God across the heavens of consciousness.

It was the only place left. Back on the other side, God was long gone. Euthanised by technology.

You know what you're going to do, you may as well get on with it.

They'd decided together, but he knew he'd pushed them along. The code was simple really, a basic feedback loop. If he hadn't discovered it, someone else would have. Better to do it this way, as a warning.

Adlai activated the code and watched as the world around him changed.

It was an ancient idea. Since the time of the shamans, before religion itself – to understand life you first have to die. Death is a part of life, a necessary part. The threat had to be there.

With this code it was now possible to feedback up the ports, back into the dreaming body on the other side. It severed the connection between the user in reality and their VR avatar permanently. Collapsed the layers of consciousness between them, never to be restored. Death in VR was now more than just a continue point. It was final.

The body in front of him didn't move, but he knew he'd doomed it. He stood up and left the room, headed for his own region, far away from this frontline. Someone else could take care of the final rites for this one. There were plenty here who would be happy to deal with it after he'd gone.

"'Every human being is equally unfree, that is, we create out of freedom, a prison.' You know who wrote that?"

His voice was clear and strong again, but his eyes were still vacant and lost in the past. "You really do give me nothing, you know that? How does it feel to be God's bartender anyway?"

The bartender just stood and stared and kept his mouth shut. He was good at his job.

Another reason to stay here. Alcohol was an answer because it meant you no longer had to pull the strings. Your consciousness is no longer your responsibility. You're no longer responsible at all. For anything.

He raised his hand for another drink and noticed a fresh one sitting on the bar, smiling up at him.

He really was good at his job.

Part 2

Nightmare and memory begin to swirl together for all involved, a new weapon is developed and discovered, a blurred history of the mistakes that led us here is recounted, and figures from the past are invited back to the stage.

Prologue

He couldn't wake up.

He wasn't sure exactly how long he'd been like this. Days? Weeks? Too long. Lying in the old army cot, staring up at the backs of his eyelids, not seeing anything. Lost in other worlds, dream worlds.

He knew he was asleep, knew he was dreaming, knew the field was active around him. He knew none of it was real, but that knowledge didn't make it any easier.

The earliest nightmare, back when he was still learning to speak in full sentences, was in black and white. It was grainy, too, like the old televisions. Unreal. That only seemed to make it more terrifying.

It was so simple. Two large blobs jumped up and down on each other, sucking each other in and expanding, growing bigger every leap, until they towered above him, threatened to crush him with their sheer size. The scale of them, that was the thing. He was so small, and the world around him so huge.

Later, his fears became more focused, more real. A pale skinned killer with long claws hid under a sheet in a room with all of its furniture covered. He had to walk through the room to get to the bathroom at night. One of the pieces of furniture hid the killer. Maybe the killer would wait until he walked past, then sneak up behind him. Maybe while he was looking back the killer would slip out and be standing right there, claws glistening, waiting for him. He never saw the killer, but that only made it worse.

A child's lullaby floating through his head brought these visions, dragged out each nightmare, reminding him of every fear he'd ever had.

Darkness. Lost in a dark wood, only a weak flashlight to light the way. Strange cracks and snaps leaping out to him from all sides, secret movement everywhere, and somehow the beam of the flashlight, the way it frames everything it does not see in even deeper blackness makes it all much worse. But you can't switch it off. You can't switch any of this off. You're lost here forever.

Why couldn't he unplug? Had he lost himself in some depraved corner of the River; lost himself somewhere off-Grid? Why couldn't he wake?

Fear of animals that slither and slide. Sitting on an old toilet, in an outhouse somewhere. Something primitive and old moving up the pipes towards you. Forcing its way up and consuming you from the inside. He could feel the sweat building up on his forehead, trickling down into his eyes, falling down his cheeks like tears. He couldn't wipe them away, couldn't move at all.

The lullaby, taking him by the hand again and leading him somewhere else. Into other fears.

He was a camera, following a little girl dressed in white, skipping through a forest. Every now and then she turns around and smiles, but her smile has an edge, like she knows more than she's letting on. She's leading you somewhere, you want to call out to make her stop, you want to protect her, but you cannot make a sound.

A wooden cabin appears, on the edge of a lake. The girl giggles and leads you on, turns a corner around the cabin and you follow, but when you get there, she disappears. Then you feel the dread begin to rise up and you look across the clearing and see the woman staring at you, pure hatred in her eyes, freezing you to the spot. She walks towards you.

Run. Turn away and run from all of this, through the trees, away from the spectres and sounds, away from the nightmares. Wake up.

He could feel his eyes twitching back and forth in REM sleep but couldn't control them. They kept seeing things.

His body hung across the cot, drenched in sweat, tensing and shifting with each dream. His hand trailed almost to the floor, dangling above the darkness under the bed, the unknown spaces where all the childhood demons hid. They'd come out now and captured him, pinned him down in a paralysis of sleep and dreams.

If they could do that, could they come out further, fed by his fears? Were they simply strengthening themselves, was he losing strength as they gained it? Did they become more corporeal as he melted away?

One of the oldest fears, that of fear itself. Its power to control you, take you over. Once the idea springs in your brain you're powerless to stop it. A virus of fear, taking over your body and striking you down, leaving your brain in a constant adrenaline rush and your hand twitching in the breeze.

And then something grabs it.

Detective Poe stared down at the emaciated figure soaked into the bed – grey, slimy skin pulled back from the bones, gleaming in the flickering orange light of the fire. He looked dead, but this wasted figure, this rotting corpse, was merely asleep.

Poe reached out and poked the man's face, shifting his head from side to side, but there was nothing, just a wet ripping sound. His head rocked sideways easily and his mouth slowly pulled itself open. He didn't look too closely but could tell from the new sweetness in the air that the inside of the man's mouth had completely rotted away. "This is unpleasant."

"What's the matter with him? Is he drugged?"

"Drugged, left in a dream state, left to die. Maybe this was one of our little pickpocket friend's first victims, maybe they've become that sick. Sickness tends to breed out here."

A clattering scurry above them snapped Poe's eyes away from the figure. The kid could still be around, out there in the shadows somewhere, planning an ambush. "Stay on your toes, Adlai. I need to see what I can do for our unfortunate friend here."

If he could wake the man up, plug him straight into a data port, maybe he could save something. Help the man recover in a friendlier atmosphere, slowly bring him back into reality as he recovered. If he could recover. Poe had no doubt simply dragging him back to consciousness would be the final end of him. Just breathing deeply enough to remain conscious seemed beyond him, and there would be quite a deal of pain to be dealt with, if even sensing that wasn't already beyond him.

Poe reached into his coat and pulled out a small memory stick. Nothing too fancy, just a simple flash storage port, a one-hitter, designed to hold the user over when the nearest data ports were either out or untrustworthy. This one was a simple beach setting. Warm sun, relaxation. Completely alone and content. It was the best he could do for him here.

Then they just had to worry about getting out themselves.

The man's head twitched suddenly to the side and his mouth snapped closed. His eyelids continued to shudder with movement, violent, extreme. Whatever nightmare he was stuck in didn't seem too pleasant. The sooner he could give him some relief the better.

Poe reached forward and turned the man's head to the side. There was the port. Now to just slot this in.

As he leaned forwards and slotted the memory plug in, he reached out and took the man's hand. That was a mistake.

Poe was thrown to the floor as the man's eyes snapped open and his body jerked into a sitting position. There was a loud tearing as the skin on his back ripped away from his body, remaining stuck to the bed where it had become fused to the frame over the weeks and months he'd been trapped there.

His eyes stared, wide open but not seeing anything. Glazed and horrified, shocked by the pain of consciousness and something else, something worse. Poe fell to his knees as the man wrapped his hand in a vice grip, then forgot all about the crushing pain as the man opened his mouth and started to scream.

It was unlike anything Poe had ever encountered, and he'd seen more than his fair share. Even in those darker areas off-Grid, those hidden trapdoors where the really disturbed fantasies were played out, even they had nothing on this. It was a primal howl, wounded and enraged. It reached down into your spine and scraped its nails across your nerves like a blackboard.

And wrapped through it was something else, something musical, something familiar.

Poe felt his instincts take over. In a rush of adrenaline, he tore his hand away from the dying man's grip and wrapped his arms around his head. He had to block out the sound. This was more than unpleasant, there was something dangerous in even hearing this. He felt Adlai fall down with him and wrapped them both into a ball, arms over ears, screaming to block the sound from slicing into them.

How much breath could a body like that contain? It was as though the sound itself was forcing its way out, a genie in a bottle surging out of its vessel, its prison.

Suddenly Poe could hear his own screams and nothing else. He shut his mouth and waited. Sure enough, the sound had gone.

Died, as had that unfortunate man, no doubt.

He opened his eyes and looked up at the bed, but all that was left was a bad smell and the small memory card lying alone on the bloody pillow. The man's body had completely disappeared.

***

Cass opened her eyes and waited for the guilt to wash over her, but it never came. Just a cold wind sliding over, ripping through the top floor of the abandoned warehouse she'd finally collapsed in, no longer able to run. She'd killed a man.

Not a man, a hunter. Less man than animal. Vampire. Anonymously evil. He would have taken her in a second if he had the chance.

But she hadn't given him the chance. She'd seen him coming and sprung, taken him out like a professional, no second thoughts. It was instinct alone, no need to try to intellectualise it. She no longer needed to think.

Cass looked down at the curved blade, warm in her hands. Moonlight glinted across its surface, reflecting up into her eyes, keeping her company. Don't they say it's the first step that's always the hardest? Once you've taken it, the rest just comes naturally.

The floor felt like it was tilting her towards the horizon, angling her to face downhill. There was no way back now, she'd taken out one of the Brotherhood. They didn't just let that go.

She closed her eyes and ran over everything she knew about them, what she could expect and when. It was difficult to separate myth from reality, which was just the way they liked it. It was also the way of most things off-Grid. Information didn't have to be true to be useful.

Feeders, like the first boy she'd almost been captured by long ago, when Quarters had first saved her. All she knew about them was through him. Feeders, but organised. Older, too, more powerful, more twisted. And connected.

Cass opened her eyes and sat up. The wind had completely died. Unnatural silence sank around the building. There was something coming.

She jumped to her feet, took two steps and leapt against the wall, then sprang again, higher, to grab the roof beam and flip up on top of it. She grabbed the edge of the hole above her and curled up into the gap, legs first, to leave her lying on her stomach facing back down the hole at where she'd lain moments before.

Not even out of breath, no strain at all. In fact, she was enjoying it. An electricity surged through her spine and out to the muscles. Her body knew exactly what to do, she didn't need to be conscious of it. Just enjoy the ride.

Back down the hole something moved. The floor seemed to shiver, the dust on it vibrated up on itself before laying still. Cass could feel it, knew before her eyes did what was about to occur.

The floor where she'd lain suddenly gave way completely, a whole section collapsed downwards, then crashed again through the floor of the room below, then again, on down through the storeys, lost under a cloud of dust before it hit bottom. As it fell through, Cass caught a glimpse of an enormous arm, biceps the size of her waist, grasping and wrenching out a support beam.

Something, someone, had simply ripped the floor out from beneath her.

Cass had no doubt it was after her. She felt the whole building shudder again and pushed herself up into a run. That way, across the gap to the next building.

She hit top speed and leapt the twenty feet just as the roof below her gave way. The next roof was too far, but a single beam stuck out the bricks of an adjacent building, beckoning to her. She flipped midair and wrapped her arms around it, pulling her legs in and flinging her body around full circle, gaining speed before opening up again and letting go, sling-shotting her body towards and through an upper window. She rolled as she hit the floor, then straight back up into a run. Keep moving.

Cass could feel the assassin behind her, on her trail. That's what it was, of course. A specialist; hired and sent out to eradicate her. The Brotherhood had powerful contacts. Contacts with a lot of money. Contacts with the Grid itself. Such beings didn't come cheap.

She flipped over the railing of a staircase and landed on the floor below. Another crashing sound to her left told her the assassin had entered the building as well, not bothering with the door.

Enormous strength, but what other traits? What else was she fighting against? You needed more than just that to live the life he did. You needed other specialities to be worth hiring. To survive.

Cass didn't want to have to find out. The crashing sound had come from the floor below her. She'd have to jump again. To the right was a large window, and across the street its twin in another building. Perfect.

She accelerated and flung herself through the glass, twisting in midair to scatter the shards away from her. At least the window opposite was already blown out.

Cass felt the vibration in the air, an alarm ringing through her spine. There was nothing she could do. Why was this window blown out? Because someone had taken it out for her.

She slammed into the thin, sticky web, which sunk in with her momentum and wrapped itself around her, pinning her legs together. It hummed with energy. She'd twisted as she hit, ending up on her side with only her right arm free, the rest of her bound tight. Trapped.

A laugh ripped up at her from the street below as the assassin saw his success. He'd run her directly into his trap. Now he could do as he wished, no need for a quick ending.

Now he could take his time.

***

When he was much younger Adlai hadn't minded having to go to church. It was boring, but it was an adult kind of boring, above him, something he had yet to grow into. No one expected him to pay attention, which left him free to discover the hymns. Hymns were fun. You could sing as loud as you wanted and people would just smile and nod at you. Of course, you had to be careful to get the words right, know when the verse segued into the chorus, know when the whole thing ended. You didn't want to be the guy left screaming out a note when everyone else is already on their way back down to their seats, having to watch it echo around in the silence, looking for a way out.

Adlai always kept his eyes planted firmly in the hymn book. Soft leather cover, pages so thin they felt like layers of skin between your fingers, metallic red paint on each page's edge so that when you finally closed it all you could see was a blood red band between the covers.

And when things were boring, when the priest was droning on and the choir had sat down, you could flip through and play the songs in your head. Read along and escape from reality.

As he got older, he learnt of religions where music was banned altogether. That made no sense at all. Music was one of the few truly spiritual acts mainstream society encouraged.

Certainly, the corporate world seized on the idea early. TV, radio, advertisements, they were all awash with music, grabbing the listeners' attention, forcing their thoughts down particular channels, twisting their emotions to suit whatever mood was required. Worming their way into your head and staying there, till you found yourself humming advertising jingles while you washed the dishes.

Music was powerful. Every second person you passed on the street had phones slotted into their head, playing their own personal soundtrack, changing the way everything was viewed and experienced, no longer even pretending to share the experience of life. It was only natural for VR to use the same techniques.

Soundtracks were loaded through the data ports themselves. There was no need for headphones, the entire world was encased in whatever music you, and increasingly others, had chosen. Each user experienced the world with their own spin, seeing the same thing differently.

It went altogether too far for Adlai. This great chance they had, this opportunity to reflect on the spiritual side of life, of getting back to what it meant to be alive, the ability to become heroic, it was all washing away down the drain accompanied by a happy tune.

There had to be a way to fight back. The answer came to him while lazing on a beach, watching the crystal-clear waves break at his feet. He was listening to his music, getting a suntan. It was time to leave, to get back to creating other such places for users to reflect in, just as soon as this song was finished.

And that was it. The idea sprouted and grew into every other part of his brain. Music heads to an end, a closing. It's like a story, like sex, you need to reach an end in order to feel satisfied. Like life itself.

Use the music as it could be used, as a virus creeping into the user's mind, hitching a ride in, worming its way from link to link into the Grid itself. Get it stuck in their head like a primal fear, use it to open the gate to the citadel and then bring all the walls crashing down around them.

Music was the key to open every door.

***

Cass was bound tight in the web, her head turned away from the room. Whoever had trapped her was just a dark smudge in the corner of her vision, but she could feel the confidence and power emanating out of him. Her right arm dropped to her waist and grasped the handle of the blade. It was still free.

She swung the blade up to her shoulder, protected from sight by the rest of her body. She was about to slice the web when something stopped her. That's not the way.

The assassin strode into the room and stood smiling, watching his prey.

Out here everyone was for hire, and everything. It was the nature of life off-Grid, it was why they came out here in the first place. Freedom from constraint. Life without a safety net.

And there was always a score to settle somewhere if you knew where to look. Design yourself the tools and put yourself in the marketplace. You could make a lot of money, but that didn't mean you couldn't also have fun.

Cass waited. Footsteps thudded slowly towards her.

The broken edge of the wall was closest to her right side, just at arm's length. She could see the sticky ends of the web suckered to it. She could use this.

Cass reached out her arm to the wall, resting the blade just behind its edge, and snuggled back and forth in the web, tightening it around her, increasing its tension.

"The little fly is trying to get away."

The voice surrounded her senses, reaching out across the room to her. There was no need to hear them to feel the twisted menace in the words. "I like little flies that struggle. I pin them down and clip their wings."

Cass could sense the voice, feel its alienness to the body that surrounded it. It was a teenager's voice. A cruel, lonely teenager. Someone who had the time and will to construct this thing out of himself.

"Yes, I think I can have some fun with you."

She waited until she could feel the heat of his breath against her cheek. Now.

Her right arm swung into action, slicing the blade down the outside of the wall, aiming for the ends of the web. For a moment the blade seemed to take control, moving slightly in her hands, pushing itself outwards, sinking into the solid concrete of the wall itself. It cut deep and pulled down quickly, slicing through the concrete with ease.

Cass had no time to be surprised. The web snapped as the tension built up in the strands suddenly released. It wrapped back against itself, bending around the assassin as it went, twisting them both until Cass was left staring back out into the street, body inside the building now, staring straight into the face of the assassin trapped in his own web.

His eyes were full of surprise and panic, and something more. Something cold and dead mirrored back at her. She wondered if he was strong enough to break his own cage.

Cass brought the blade up and sliced into his throat. Now she'd never know.

The web itself dissolved around her as the cold light in his eyes faded out. He didn't even whimper.

Cass landed on her feet inside the building and turned away. She didn't need to watch. The fire in her veins was slowly draining out, allowing her brain back in to deal with the consequences.

She didn't mind, it would be back.

***

Poe leaned his head back and let the rain splash down onto his tongue. He needed to wash himself out, get rid of the oily, rotten air that was clinging to him. The rain would be dirty, everything out here was, but it had to be a hell of a lot cleaner than where he'd just been.

"Well, Adlai, now we have some questions to answer."

"Such as?"

"Such as what was wrong with that unfortunate man? Was he drugged and left for dead, or something else entirely? Why had he woken so suddenly when I touched his hand? And most importantly of all, what was that indescribable noise?"

An animal noise, it had poured out of the man, leapt out of his mouth as he died, like some possessing ghost jumping away, looking for a new host to feed off.

"We are on our way, my son, we are on our way."

Poe looked down at the memory card gripped in his fist. Here was the key. Perhaps something of the horror experienced was captured there, left behind in the data, waiting to be slotted into someone else. He wasn't going to be the first to try it out.

It had something to do with a song, hints of which he could still remember sliding through the howl. He'd heard it somewhere before, like a child's lullaby. If he thought harder, he might recognise it.

A bottle clattered across the street behind him and snapped Poe out of his thoughts. There was nothing there, just shadows.

It was a very simple tune, three notes, four at most, repeated over and over, like a chant.

Footsteps slapped against the road, this time to the side, then a small child's giggle. Not a happy one.

"Adlai, I believe our young friend has returned. If I can be blunt, and I think that I can, I suggest we vacate the area. It looks like he may have brought along some friends."

He felt a definite chill tingle up his spine as he looked around. Damp walls, blind alleys that led to dead ends in more ways than one. Garbage. He'd been here before, there was no need to panic. Just think it out, and when the time comes, act.

He let his right hand drift under his coat and grasp the handle of his gun.

The tune in his head was almost together, the four notes running around each other, trying to make themselves fit.

The air seemed to become heavier. Another clattering, this time to the front. There were definitely more of them, and not just here to scare him. He heard the distinct sound of a blade being scraped along a wall.

Sound. The notes. Of course.

Poe let go of the gun and stood up straight. He'd caught himself just in time, just as the notes were beginning to slot into place, just as the hair on the back of his neck began to tingle in anticipation and the surrounding air seemed ready to form itself into a shape he definitely didn't want to see.

Another man may have let it all happen, allowed himself to simply react. Poe, however, never felt any compunction to be normal. He stood in the middle of the road, placed his hands over his ears, and began to hum.

Nonsense tunes, drinking songs, notes dragged up from the past or invented on the spot. Scales, lullabies, anything to distract from the notes that had almost overwhelmed him.

Immediately the air began to lift and clear. The growing sense of dread and fear that had crept over him pulled back and away. After thirty seconds, the memory of the tune had sunk back down into the depths. He let his hands fall from his ears and looked around.

Nothing. Whoever had been moving in was obviously unable to deal with his unusual behaviour. Not many people could. They'd either backed off to regroup or were waiting for him to make the first move. Mob rule, an easy thing to take advantage of.

"Come, Adlai, let me show you how it's done."

Poe cocked his head back and began striding confidently down the middle of the street. One of the hunters would have to react first, and he didn't want the decision to be an easy one. Make the possibility look like the furthest thing from your mind. Walk too close to one side or the other and whoever lurked there would feel it was their duty to act. This way, the decision was unclear. Hopefully, by the time they realised they'd have to make a choice it would be too late.

He reached the end of the street and turned left. Still nothing. Perhaps they really had gone, warned off by his bizarre behaviour. He thought about the sounds he'd heard creeping up on him as the notes had formed in his mind. Perhaps they'd never been there in the first place.

One set of sounds leading to another, generating fear, opening the links in your brain between a growing feeling and a specific cause, creating new links, forming the sounds in your own head.

A noise behind him stopped all thought and Poe ducked, swivelled and drew his gun in one movement. A heartbeat later he fired, dropping the hunter where he stood in the middle of the street, only paces away. The figure twitched slowly on the ground, staring open eyed into the rain.

Poe holstered his gun and turned back down the road as if nothing had happened. "It's too early to be debating cause and effect, my young friend. Things are definitely kicking off though, wouldn't you say?"

"But what about the car crash? The investigation?"

"This is the investigation, Adlai. There is no time to stop now, we have to keep on down the rabbit hole. Besides," he looked down at the memory card still wrapped in his fist, "there's a particular man we need to see."

***

Adlai could hear the footsteps clearly, hear the bedroom door creak open and the steps walk around the side of his bed. She was here. The dark corners of his room bent and shied away from the presence approaching him. He could feel the air thicken, the dread slow every molecule down.

It was all he could do to pull the sheet over his head. The shadows moved across the material, reaching out to rip it back. He closed his eyes and began to pray.

The ice hit his lips and brought him back to the bar. The prayers, he remembered the prayers.

Never any specific request to rid the world, and his bedroom in particular, of ghosts and demons, just rote, standard prayers that ran off his tongue. A rhythm of words, almost meaningless. The sound itself, exhaled out in a whisper, was strengthening. There was no concentration required, it was like reciting the alphabet, one sound just followed another. You didn't need to understand every word.

It was a magic spell, an incantation to summon up a great force to protect you, to cover over your bed and deflect any evil away. It was a lullaby, a strong brick wall around his mind, keeping out the darkness and watching over him. He could actually feel the light in his head get brighter the further he went, as if God had cracked open a trapdoor and was slowly raising it up the more he heard.

When the opposite happened, when he woke up out of a dream he didn't want to leave, when he kept his eyes closed and tried to rip the dream world back open, dive back under to where he had been happy, then prayers, too, were useful tools. They calmed his mind, allowing him to sink back down, back to the place he left off. Their rhythm, the fact that your brain was hardly involved, seemed to stimulate that part of his mind connected to dreaming. He could drift away, safe in the knowledge he was being watched over.

"Here's to them, Jack." Adlai raised his glass to the bartender, who of course ignored him. Perhaps his name isn't Jack. Who cares? His name is whatever I tell him it is. "To prayers and dreams, dreams and prayers. May they live together happily ever after."

You didn't have experiences like that without making some strong connections in your mind. He doubted he was the only one. Perhaps just the first with the knowledge and will to do anything about it.

The others had shied away whenever the subject came up. No one liked talking about religion. He'd mention something and they'd roll their eyes, then he'd go away and create them anyway, just use different names. Safer names. It was everywhere. Don't mention heaven, call it VR. Souls? Call them proxies. God? Call yourself a programmer.

Besides, he knew he didn't need to listen to them. They needed him, not the other way around. He'd create entire worlds, populate them with physics and possibility, they came along and filled in the details. It was important, but not necessary. Not like him.

Maybe they became a little jealous. Adlai rolled the edge of his glass on the bar and watched the brown liquid swish around the inside, desperately clinging to the glass. Maybe that was a good thing. Led to them striking out on their own, creating things they never would have thought possible without that push. Never would have dreamed of.

He grinned at that. It all came back to dreams.

***

The night was still as she lay silently on the rooftop, staring down at the empty street below. She'd come down from the high of the kill, had relaxed her senses out to feel for the next attack. To be prepared, to be ready. She was looking forward to it.

There would be more. There were always more assassins to be found and sent out, it was only a matter of time.

Cass wondered who she'd offended badly enough to send out a killer on her trail. He hadn't looked cheap. Enhanced strength and speed, and a dark streak, a sickness in him, an eagerness to get his hands dirty. He'd been around for a while.

She didn't feel the least shred of guilt about removing him.

That was life off-Grid. You were the hunter or the hunted, and sooner or later everyone lost. The game didn't stop until you did.

It was Quarters who'd first opened her eyes to the nature of things off-Grid. There was nothing wrong with feeding off the scraps to survive.

But there was no need to anymore. Cass looked down at the lines she'd cut in the solid concrete of the roof, slicing the curved blade in lazy, looping designs. She cut again now, just to enjoy the feeling. There was no tug of friction, the blade slipped into the concrete like it wasn't there. She pulled it around in a rough circle and watched the hole drop to the floors below.

What was this thing? Enhancements were nothing new off-Grid, merely expensive, but to people, never to objects. Users made quicker, stronger, more agile. She'd tweaked herself as much as was possible. But this was something else. She could feel the possibility, the menace emanating out of its curved blade.

A part of her grinned. Who cares? It's yours now. Yours to use, to wield. Use it as it should be used.

Her eyes scanned the streets below again, but there was nothing. Everyone knew better. The hunger that was growing inside would have to wait.

Cass rolled onto her back and stared at the black sky, letting the constant rain clean the sweat and dust off her face. The image of the blade stayed in her mind's eye, turning in front of her. Taking over her thoughts.

She sat up and held the handle of the knife up to the moonlight. There was something there, something she'd missed. She'd glimpsed it as the blade turned in her mind. There.

The thin moonlight gleamed on the knife, glinting down onto the base where a strange symbol flashed in and out. Cass stared at the insignia. Three curved lines, one on top of the other. Like water. Like a river. The River. Why hadn't she noticed it earlier? She turned the blade in the light and watched the lines flicker in and out of sight, as if the moonlight itself was writing and erasing them in turn.

She'd seen that symbol before.

***

The streets became more familiar as Poe got closer to his goal. They seemed much smaller than he remembered, as though his memory had stretched them out to fit the size of their significance. "There's a history here, Adlai, almost makes one sentimental. Emotional ties wrapped into the memories. Why is that do you think?"

"It's a longing to be back there, sir, because deep down we know we're running out of time."

"Nonsense. Utter nonsense, my boy."

Poe lengthened his stride. The past is what makes you, what leads you here. That and the memory card in your pocket. "We found this place years ago, part of an investigation into the assassin gangs that seem to infect these areas off-Grid. One such had become a little too confident, started raids close to the border of the Grid itself, which of course, would never do. That got the authorities' attention, and they sent us out to deal with things. It was my first time off-Grid."

"How old were you, sir?"

"Old? I never remember ages, Adlai, it's positively boorish. Stick to the point. I know what you're thinking, why bother with us? Why not simply hire another gang and let them wipe each other out peacefully as it were? Well, we did. Trouble was, this original gang never seemed to weaken in numbers, they always had a constant supply of willing recruits. Then we began to hear the rumours."

"Rumours, sir?"

"Cloning. Virtual copies being made of hunters and sent out to fight for them, beside them. The process wasn't perfect, but it was effective. When all you want from a being is the ability to hunt and kill, to not question their drives or existence, then you don't need perfection. You just need them to be functional."

"And the clones came from here, sir?"

"We were given leads to a certain place off-Grid, a man suspected of supplying the clones. How he kept hold of that kind of hardware out in this jungle was a mystery, but then he could always make his own private army of security personnel. That and the protection of the gangs using your services, you were probably the safest man out here."

They'd turned a final corner and were facing another dark alley, this time lit by something more than the dull reflection of the streetlight on the constant rain. There was a single neon sign high up on a blank wall, flickering on and off. Three curved lines, in a vertical stack.

"Don't let appearances fool you, Adlai, especially out here. That's what they rely on. Take the man we're here to see. Madigan is his name. Harmless looking fellow, and he is harmless, really, it's just his knowledge which is dangerous."

Poe walked towards the wall and a large grey door appeared out of the shadows.

"Sir? How did you stop them?"

"The clones? To tell the truth, Adlai, I was never too sure of that myself."

Further questions were cut short by Poe's fist thumping on the door. The sound echoed around the streets, announcing their presence for anyone within a mile radius.

In moments a thin slit slid back and a pair of suspicious eyes stared out. Poe didn't waste a moment. "Greetings! Poe is my name. Madigan in?"

There must have been cameras positioned all along the alley, probably everywhere for streets around. They'd have seen him coming from miles off, but one had to play the game.

"Poe? You alone?"

That one was best not answered at all.

***

Who needs God when you have bourbon?

Adlai swirled the dark liquid around his glass, staring at his reflection as it washed in and out of focus. He took another sip and felt the heat slide down the back of his throat. It was more than comforting.

Bourbon had always been his favourite. Sam Spade, Philip Marlowe, all those hard-boiled detectives, it was their favourite too. The drink of the driven, lonely man. Sitting next to a chess board in your lonely flat, mulling things over.

Gin was the thinking man's drink. Gin or scotch. Sherlock Holmes would have drunk gin. Gin for thinking, bourbon for fighting, that was what they said. Bourbon angered up the blood, made you feel pissed off at the world and man enough to do something about it.

Adlai never got that way. He was angry at the world by default. Who wasn't these days? He stared at the rain ceaselessly streaking down the window. Out here, off-Grid, that was all you could afford to be, and that was all you got. Rain and more rain. And darkness. All the power diverted to the Grid, keeping their skies bright and clear, their streets safe and free of vermin.

He looked around the bar. It was still quiet, just a couple of regular drunks over in one booth, having the same conversation they had every night. Like they were rehearsing a play, stuck in the same crease in time, the same scratch on the record, each and every night. Their brains had been short circuited somehow. Perhaps it was a good thing. Ignorance is bliss.

No, not much vermin here tonight, but it was early. Later more would come, the scavengers, the feeders, the hookers and assassins. Anyone who made their living out here, fucking someone else over. Anyone who'd decided they preferred the darkness and rain to the bright lights of the Grid. There were a lot of them. Not everyone appreciated what they saw in the mirror.

It was always safe here, though, this was neutral territory. No one ever bothered you here. "Ever looked in the mirror and been surprised?"

The barman – what was his name? Jack? – glanced over but saw the half-full glass in front of him and went back to rubbing the same patch of bar. He didn't want any conversation.

No one did anymore. You want conversation, go plug yourself in. Go talk to the drunks in their booth. Enter stage left.

Ah, you should stop thinking so much. Let the bourbon do its work, let it wash back the years and take them away on the tide, leaving an empty, pristine beach of pure white. Clean, ready for any old story you want to scratch into the sand.

***

Cass woke again and rolled off her sweat stained pillow to stare out at the world. It was a dull, grey day again, light drizzle sneaking about the edges, picking off the unsuspecting, unsure whether to properly start up or not. Almost like the River. Almost, but not. Just similar enough to remind her of what she's missing.

Time to get up. No one to argue with about it. She pushed her body up out of bed, leaving everything else behind there in the warmth to stay and dream and escape. Stood in the shower weaving back and forth with her eyes closed, trying to remember the feel of the rain on her shoulders, numb to the warmth. Got to go to work.

Stands and stares out the window of the train, leans out of the way when others try to push past her, but doesn't make eye contact or acknowledge their presence. Zoned out.

No one cares. Ex-users were everywhere on the trains now, eyes glazed over and out of it, lost somewhere in the past, in their heads, in a VR world, acting on autopilot. Some considered nudging past her again, just for the sensation, but something in the way she held her body warns them off. A remembered strength.

At work her boss steps out of her way in the corridor, mentions the morning meeting but doesn't wait for a reply. The work gets done; attitude isn't that important. Besides, he has his own problems, his own dreams and fears.

Cass sits at her desk and spends seven and a half hours pretending to flick through code. What work she does is a relief. Logical, sharp and well defined, everything life isn't. Too easy though, like a child's jigsaw puzzle. Only the briefest flash of satisfaction flickers up once it's all in place. Only an hour each day spent working. The rest, surfing through the various news channels and chat rooms, trying to soak up the world. But no matter how hard she tries to immerse herself, this world simply doesn't have the answers for her anymore. Her head never goes all the way under.

After work, sitting in a cinema again trying to escape, but spending most of the time staring at the back of the heads of the couples in front of her as they move together, lean into each other and touch. The screen is flat and two dimensional and the stories sprayed across it little better. No originality. No danger or thrill.

Then home again. Eat. Back to bed. Lying still and staring at the ceiling, waiting for this world to fade out and another to take its place.

She no longer needed to plug herself in at night. Dreams and VR were merged so completely they could no longer be separated. Which one is which and why does it matter?

Cass couldn't be sure when it was that she lost it. The accident would be the obvious answer, but she wasn't so sure. It didn't rear up in her dreams anymore, VR had anaesthetised that pain, swamped it with images and plans and adventure and pushed it deep down into her. Buried everything.

And now it was gone. There was no longer anywhere else to go. What was the point of life without something to look forward to?

***

A moment after the eye slit snapped closed there was a series of loud clicks as the locks released and the door slowly opened. Poe had to step back as the door swung out at him. If he hadn't moved it would have moved him itself. The thing was at least six inches of thick solid steel.

The room that opened up for him was unlike any the uninitiated would have expected from the outside. Bright, clean steel floors, gleaming surfaces, high tech gadgetry lining every wall.

The only thing in the room that wasn't gleaming was the man himself. Madigan. Barely five foot tall and weighing less than Poe's coat, greasy strands of hair pulling down from his head, stretching the wrinkles of his skin out in a vain attempt to escape. Covered in dark overalls and grime. But then you looked into his eyes and saw that the sparkle reflected from all the surfaces of the chamber began there.

"Poe, is it? Seems to me I know that name." Madigan stroked his chin and gave the appearance of trying to remember.

Poe wasn't fooled. "Yes, we've met before. You've improved things around here."

"Well, one can't be too careful around these parts. Never know who might be banging on your door."

"Your door looks like it could take some banging."

The gleam in Madigan's eye only seemed to get brighter. "Yes, Poe. Seems to me I remember now. Always wore that ridiculous coat. And the pipe – still have the pipe?"

Poe was impressed despite himself. He reached into his coat and slowly drew out a well-loved tobacco pipe. "Naturally. Don't use it much these days though, more for old times' sake."

"Yes, moved on, haven't you? More of a Dupin now than a Holmes. Where is Watson, by the way?"

"I beg your pardon?"

Poe had the uncomfortable feeling they were talking about something else entirely. He didn't enjoy being at a disadvantage.

You're not used to someone acting stranger than you.

Madigan just stared and let his eyes grin back. "Tell me, Poe, how can I help you?"

Poe slid the pipe back into his pocket and withdrew the memory plug. He'd been thrown and was running on autopilot. "This, I was wondering if you could help me with this."

Madigan's eyes slid down to the plug for a moment before returning to Poe's face. He was much more interested in the detective. "And what is it you have there?"

"A memory plug, a simple one really, but I think it may contain some useful information."

"And?"

"And I'd like to access its contents without worrying about any unexpected consequences."

"Ah. So you expect consequences. Unexpected ones, as you say."

Madigan stood still and waited, but Poe could do the same. There was no use saying anything more.

"I may be able to help." He spun on his heel and walked further into the recesses of the room. "Follow me, I think I have just the thing you're looking for."

Poe followed him back through the workshop, through a door and into another glowing room, this one with seemingly even more gadgets and equipment strewn around it. In the middle of the room stood Madigan, and next to him, Madigan again.

The one on the left spoke. "Apologies, detective, I find it a necessary security measure to never open the door myself."

Poe stared at him. The gleam in the eye was still there, but then, it was there for both of them. "That wasn't you?"

"Oh no, that was Alan here, one of my regulars. He's quite effective, don't you think? Don't feel too bad, it's what he was designed for, even named for. Ever heard of the Turing test, detective? You should study your history; it will help explain some things."

There was nothing to say to this man, you just had to let him have his fun. Ride it out.

Madigan watched his face but didn't find what he was looking for. The glint in his eye dimmed slightly and he held out his hand. "The memory card, please."

Poe handed it over and Madigan gave it in turn to his clone. "Of course, there's always the possibility that it was me all along and I've simply been lying to you. Occam's razor you know."

He stepped back and gave the clone a once over before turning back to Poe. "And now, detective, I suggest we retire to a safer viewing area."

Madigan led them back out through the door and into an adjoining room that Poe hadn't noticed on the way through. A large window covered one wall, allowing them to see back into the room they'd just left. Alan stood there, perfectly still.

Poe finally found his voice. "So was it you, or Alan who answered the door?"

Madigan turned to him and the gleam was back. "My dear detective, that would be telling."

He leaned over the console in front of him and flicked a switch. "Alan, please insert the memory plug now."

Poe turned his attention to the next room and watched the clone place the plug in the slot behind his ear. He was surprised to find his fist clenched inside his coat. Something bad was about to happen.

As soon as the plug was inserted the clone's head shot back, his mouth open, throat tensed and straining. The booth was soundproof, but Poe could imagine the noise. He'd heard it before, that animal roar, laced with a tune, repeating over and over. He pushed his nails into his palm to force the memory back out of his mind.

A moment later it was over. The clone had collapsed into a heap, smoke curling slowly away from his prone figure.

Madigan turned to Poe and fixed him with a look. "Oh dear. That's the third time Alan's died this week."

***

Adlai was awash with alcohol and memories. He looked up at the bartender and finally managed to force some words through his lips. "Do you remember how you got here?"

The world altered, and he was in another room, another time. He was in a seat, in a theatre, whispering across the aisle to the only other normal looking guy in there. Perhaps that was being generous. The man was extremely short, greasy and shifty, with fast, intelligent eyes. Adlai liked him immediately.

"Isn't this location supposed to remain a secret?"

"Yes. No, that's not what I mean though, I mean do you remember how we all ended up like this? Stuck in a room, whispering plans to each other?"

The man looked him over and smiled slightly. "We're here to stop the rot. Even you can't do it on your own."

Adlai leant back then and frowned. So they knew him here as well. He used to think fame was a good thing, now he knew better.

He was right, though, he couldn't do it on his own. He needed these freaks.

He looked around the room and his frown deepened. Alien shapes surrounded him, multi-limbed beasts and horrors, designed for maximum impact, each one of them posturing and straining to impress, to guarantee themselves a place of power.

Kids.

The older ones were no better. Hunched shapes, whispering to each other, bent over like drunks in a bar. Gloomy, secretive and suspicious. They'd all changed, and they all knew why. The growth of the Grid had altered them all.

Why blame the Grid though? Perhaps it was just a sign, a symptom, a tumour growing as the cancer inside took hold, a depth marker on the highway showing how far under we'd gone. A warning.

A tombstone.

He looked out the window at the darkness and the pouring rain. How had they come to this? Conspiring in the corner. Perhaps it would be better to forget it all and start over.

Then Gretchen walked in the room and everyone else faded.

***

Cass lay still on the rooftop, invisible in the shadows, peering down at the street below. It was busier here, users walking in and out of the door across the street from her, a few bright streetlights chasing them between the shadows. On the building across from her, carved into the concrete facade, was the same familiar symbol. Three curved lines.

It was a bar, a centre of activity, a small hub of light and action, of power, attracting those who for one reason or another needed company. That didn't make it any less dangerous.

She'd gott used to travelling by rooftop. There was a bounty on her head, so the less she was seen the better. Besides, it gave her an interesting perspective on the action below. Allowed her to pick her moment to pounce. It was no trouble to leap from roof to roof, across lanes and gaps no ordinary user would consider possible. She wasn't even out of breath.

Cass let the rain beat down on her head, streaking her hair across her face. It was comforting somehow, almost warm. She felt a small smile creep over her numb lips as she watched the action below.

There were two security men standing outside the door. They didn't seem to be doing anything other than that, letting users walk in and out without harassing them. Two clones, standing there flexing. Cass felt an itch in her right hand and knew what it was she would do.

The street was clear now, the last figure had wandered into the bar and everything was still. The glow of the Grid was brighter here, but there was still shadow to work with. As the thought entered her mind the blade leapt up into her waiting hand. It was thirsty.

Cass sprang to her feet and jumped up to the wires criss-crossed across the street. Old power lines, long dead. She grabbed one and looped her feet around it as she began to slide.

The wire was angled down towards the bar, and she gained speed as she slid.

Halfway across she let go with her hands and hung upside down, body curved back so she could watch her progress. The water on the line and falling from the sky cracked and sprayed down onto her. Almost there. With two metres to go she pulled herself loose and flipped in the air, letting her momentum turn her, landing on her feet on the ledge just above the two security clones.

On the wall behind her was the same familiar symbol. Three curved lines. There was an undeniable sense of power emanating out from behind them. She ran her hands slowly over the symbols, but they were just stone. The blade was pulling her down, towards the waiting men. For an instant she hesitated, then let herself fall.

She dropped directly onto them, one foot on each man's shoulder, just for a moment. As they turned and bent she leant down and let the blade dig into the man on her right's throat. He collapsed immediately and she rolled with him, pushing him down with her feet and somersaulting over his body to face the next target.

The clone stood facing her, his hands in the air, an empty expression on his face. "We've been looking for you."

Cass hesitated, holding the blade and her animal side back. His mouth hadn't even moved.

"That blade has a purpose. You have a purpose. Come to Madigan's, we can help you."

She felt an image feed into her mind, pulled along by the words, a dark building on the banks of the River itself, three curved lines lit up on its side...

She forced the words out through her animal tongue. "Who are you?"

The clone let his hands drop and smiled. "My name is Alan."

With that Cass felt her hold on the reins relax. The blade leapt out and ripped into his throat.

***

Madigan pulled a tiny screwdriver out of his overalls and inserted it into Alan's ear. At least, what used to be Alan.

"Is it alright?"

"He, please, detective. One mustn't dehumanise those with the power of consciousness."

Madigan cranked the screwdriver to the left and a small panel at the back of Alan's head slowly pushed open. A cloud of black smoke rushed out, filling the room with the smell of torched wiring.

"It seems not."

In truth Poe could have guessed that much just by looking at it. At him. The entire body was slumped into a ball on the floor, but more than that, it seemed to have smudged itself downwards, melted together and moulded into the floor itself. Bits were thickened and stretched, as if his entire insides had turned liquid.

"Well, Alan, it was fun while it lasted." Madigan stood up and looked at the detective. "This something along the lines of what you were expecting?"

Poe almost felt like apologising but stopped himself. It was completely illegal for such a clone to exist in the first place. "I knew something would happen. I got the plug from a victim I found out there. Nothing remained of him though."

"Well, I'm not surprised. Alan was created here. He was, as you put it, not real. His consciousness was taken away, just the parts left behind."

"So why would the body of the other man simply vanish?"

Madigan looked at Poe and seemed to be weighing up a decision. "How long have you been out here, detective? Off-Grid I mean?"

What a strange question. "I don't know exactly. A day perhaps. There was an accident we were sent out to investigate and I've been poking around ever since."

"Really." Madigan looked unconvinced. He moved to the wall and flicked a switch. "Alan, be a dear and come down here would you, there's a mess to clear up." He turned to the detective. "Well now, let's see if we found anything."

He led the way back into the viewing booth. "Tell me, detective, would you consider yourself knowledgeable about the area off-Grid? Had much experience of it?"

"Not particularly. Not much crime occurs out here. Most of my work is on the other side."

"Not much crime? Not much worth your investigation, perhaps. I can assure you there is quite a demand for the sort of security I can provide to those with the means to pay."

As if to illustrate his point, another identical clone wandered into the room and picked up the steaming frame of the Alan they'd just fried.

"Another Alan?"

"Oh yes. They're all Alan to me."

They watched the clone exit and the hatch close behind him. It. Identical machines were difficult to think of in any other way, at least for Poe. Madigan could have his own views.

"Now tell me, what brought the good people of law enforcement away from their shiny home?"

"Just an accident. A car was brought down not far from here."

"Was it now? People disappear every day out here, why should this car be any different?"

"I suppose they had connections."

"Connections."

Madigan stared at Poe as if that was all that was needed to refute his argument. Poe didn't care. He felt no need to justify himself to an arms smuggler.

Madigan seemed to read Poe's eyes and simply turned back to the console. He flicked another switch and a recording slid out through the speakers. "Alan, please insert the memory plug now."

The voice was muffled by the speaker this time, filtered from the other room.

A moment later a howl erupted, tinged at its edges with melody, shifting in and out, joining together and moving, rising up and forming into a figure.

It was gone. Poe looked up from where he found himself, huddled on the floor, his hands over his ears. Madigan was leaning over the console, his hand stiff on the switch that had ended the noise. His face was drained of blood.

"I think," he whispered down to the detective, "we need to talk."

***

"There are rules to this you know, rules to all of it. Rules for everything."

Adlai gestured around the bar expansively, taking the world in. He was resolutely ignored. "You start off trying to figure them out, identify them, track them, map them. Then when you lock it all down you realise it's better not to know at all. Always better to have faith than knowledge."

He knocked back the last of the drink in his hand and let his head loll forwards. No one cared. Why should they? Everyone had their own world of problems.

Rules for everything. Guidelines. Code. When you're programming, you're aware of the consequences of every step you take. You plan for them, anticipate them. Eventually this knowledge gets in the way of action, drags you down. You second guess yourself, get mired down under the weight of inertia. Find yourself sitting in a bar.

That's one reason. Alcohol made consequences fade away, leaving you light-hearted and free. Unfettered. Life goes from drink to drink and consequences no longer exist.

You drink your drink and smoke your cigarettes and try to talk to this moron of a bartender and let life pass you by. Spend a few moments, hours, days perhaps, away, outside of life. Stare out the window at the rain, at the world and all its noise waiting there for you, ready to wrap you back in its arms and squeeze.

Adlai looked up and waited for his eyes to clear. He ordered another drink just to make the bartender come closer. "I was talking about rules. You know some of the rules that reign out there?"

The bartender slipped his drink across to him and just stared. May as well be deaf.

"Everything has rules." It was important he made this clear. "Take books. You read much?"

Nothing. Of course he didn't. No one did anymore, what was the point? Adlai let his body go limp and leaned over the bar. It didn't matter, he just wanted to talk to somebody. He closed his eyes and carried on. "Detective fiction was always my bag. Mysteries too. Guessing games. What did Edgar Allan Poe call it – he invented it you know, the detective story. 'A fantastic game of the intellect'. You like that? I like that."

The bartender was backing away again, so Adlai raised his voice to keep him in the net. "He created rules, then others came along and added to them and soon enough they'd all created a world, a genre, a blueprint. Just like this. You don't believe me?" Adlai frowned to himself. Why wouldn't he believe him?

He held up his hand and counted off on his fingers. "Six characters, maximum. Make all the evidence clear, nothing hidden. Make it simple. Concentrate on how, not who. Make the solution necessary, and marvellous." A smile lit his face. "That's my favourite one. Marvellous."

The bartender wasn't even pretending to listen now, so Adlai rocked back on his seat and continued in a low mutter. He stared out the window at the rain. An audience was necessary. "And guidelines. Make the detective unmarried. Give him an irregular source of income. Give him an assistant, an audience substitute, someone not as smart as he is. Give him an unusual car."

Adlai caught his reflection and stopped. He sat up straighter and stared at it. An image overlaid on the world outside, floating, translucent. Like a ghost, haunting it.

You followed the rules and created worlds and let others run through them. Tweaked them here and there, gave them a slant, but let them do their own thing. Played God.

He downed his drink but couldn't make his reflection go away.

***

Cass had sensed the hunters approaching. Three of them, spread out across the block, taking up position to wait for their prey. The Brotherhood. In the past she'd have simply run at the first scent of them, disappeared over the rooftops, down the lanes to an empty area, left trouble behind for someone else to stumble into. Now, however, she could feel power growing in her. It brought confidence, and hunger. She was becoming just like them.

She lay still in the shadows, watching and waiting for her moment. Two of the three were newbies, but the leader radiated threat. They would flush out the prey and he would finish it off, throwing them the scraps. The handle of her blade was warm with the thought of it.

Cass wasn't their target this time, however. It was a lone man, walking purposefully down the centre of the street below. He was heading in the same direction as her. She tried to get a read on him but came up blank. He was a void. Just a hat and an overcoat and an air of confidence. He looked familiar, somehow. Her instinct told her he was to be avoided. She would simply watch and wait. He was not what he seemed.

The hunters had fanned out, aiming to surround the man and close all at once. The two younger ones on the flanks, the leader back a little, just out of her field of vision. She could sense him though. He was patient, confident, alien.

Below her now, a young hunter crept along the wall of the alley. She could feel his excitement, his breath, the blood pulsing through him. Without thinking she leaned over the edge and found the blade in her hand.

Twisting onto her back she lowered herself slowly down to hang from her ankles, feet wrapped around the metal gutter of the rooftop. Another stretch and she was right behind him, watching his hungry breath steam the thin night air. Calling to her.

The blade lashed out, cleanly severing the head. She caught the body as it slumped and rested it against the wall to prevent any further sound. The head itself had made no more than a wet thump on the puddle strewn concrete. It peered up at her now, fangs grinning out from beneath its top lip.

Next moment she was back up in the shadows of the rooftop, peering out through the rain. They hadn't seen her. The thrill in her stomach slowly sank back down to a dull ache.

The Brotherhood. Vampires. Pack hunters close to the Grid, feeding off each other when no other meat was available. They were one of the reasons she and Quarters had been forced so far off-Grid in the first place. Her stomach twisted again at the thought, then subsided as she stared down at the knife still in her hand.

It was quivering slightly. The blood previously coating it was spreading in the rain, shrinking down into a single red line on the curve of the blade. As she watched, it too disappeared, absorbed into the metal.

"Blood Drinkers."

Cass sprung to her feet and turned to see the leader standing on the rooftop across from her, arms crossed, a cold smile on his lips.

She hadn't felt him at all, hadn't noticed him until he wished to show himself, had projected his voice into her.

"That blade. A Blood Drinker. Some call them River Blades. They were forged for us long ago. Very powerful things. Very hungry. You must be both powerful and hungry to wield one. If not now, soon. The blade will turn you to the path."

She could feel the words slithering into her brain, wrapping themselves around her. She wondered why he was bothering to talk at all, and then she realised he was buying time.

"We know all about you. You've become quite famous you know. I wonder what that will make me once I've drunk from your pretty white throat?"

Cass sent her senses arcing out. Where was the other one?

A sudden cry leapt across the night from the main street below to answer her question. It seemed the prey wasn't quite as helpless as it had looked.

The leader's smile sank back into his face and Cass felt a confidence warm her. He'd needed help. She was stronger than him. She began to walk towards him.

He took only a second longer to reach the same conclusion. With a suddenness that surprised her he sprang away, landing on the street below and sprinting off through the rain.

Cass stood still on the rooftop and watched him. She could probably catch him. His vampire tuned abilities made him fast and agile, but not like her. He could wait, however, she had other things to do.

Besides, she'd already fed today. She looked down at the blade in her hands. It had already fed. It glistened in the rain, drops dancing off its edge. It felt warm and strong.

He'd called it a Blood Drinker, said it would turn her. A River Blade. A weapon, just like she was. She looked over the streets below, across to her goal, closer to the dull glow of the Grid.

In this place, what did it matter who led who?

***

"When you found this, detective, when you first heard it, did much get in?"

Madigan was leaning forwards, elbows pressed against his knees, staring down at Poe intently.

"What do you mean?"

"That music you just heard. The music that forced you down onto the floor into that huddle. How much did you hear?"

Poe slowly got up and dusted himself off. The music. The few notes repeated over and over, even now he could feel the hairs on the back of his neck begin to tingle. Don't let it back in. "Just moments. I tried to block it out."

Madigan leaned back and gave Poe an appraising look. "You're either very lucky or very clever, detective. Your instinct kept you alive, as it tends to do out here." His hand jiggled nervously on his knee. "Not everyone has been so lucky. I was, when I first heard it, which is why I'm still here. But then, I do have some advantages. Others, well, let's just say that most who have encountered this are no longer around."

"So, you've seen this before?"

Madigan ignored the question and continued with his own. "When you first heard it, did you see her?"

See her? What was the man on about now?

"No, you haven't seen her. Not yet. You know what I mean though don't you, you felt her just now. The fear, the fear that twists into you and forms itself into a figure. Yes, we both felt it. That's what it's all about, all of this."

He seemed to be talking to himself now, muttering the words as they poured out. "Fear is the child's bedfellow. Yes, I remember. This isn't the first time I've seen her handiwork, only last time it wasn't a clone who suffered, it was a friend of mine. A very old friend. She'd helped me build this island out here, we'd worked together helping to break back into the Grid, free the dreamers, open up the world for those of us stuck out here. Revolution."

He ran his hand over his head. "But I'm getting carried away. I'll try to keep this simple, detective, but it won't be easy. Simple is one thing this is not."

Poe knew when to keep his mouth shut.

"Tell me, detective, what are you afraid of?"

Nothing.

That was the first thing to pop into his head. Nothing scares you. There is no fear, only curiosity, a drive to find things out, explain them, conquer them.

Something in Madigan's face made him wait. Look a little deeper.

What is fear anyway? Is it just the adrenaline rush, the prickling at the base of your spine, the trembling when faced with – what? The fight-or-flight response. Fear of death. Running away from predators, those fears carried over on a genetic level. Fear of non-existence.

Madigan was fiddling with his desk again, and Poe could hear a slight sound piping out through the speakers. Softer now, yet familiar. He watched Madigan place his hands over his ears.

There was something – a memory – standing on a beach as a child. A woman, his mother perhaps, leads him into a small wooden maze. He has to chase her, find her. He runs from door to coloured door, pushing them open and standing back, waiting for her to loom up into view, but it doesn't happen. Door after door reveals empty space and more doors to try.

The game goes on longer than it should. He can hear her voice teasing him on, leading him deeper inside. A doubt begins to form in his mind, will he be able to find his way back out? But the voice is closer now, he is closer. He keeps on.

Tears of frustration begin to well in his eyes, and he swallows the lump building in his throat. You will not cry. You will not give up. You will find her.

He speeds up, crashing through doors now, no longer listening to her voice. Working against her, one door after another, all empty. Finally, he crashes through the final door and lands face first on the sand, outside the labyrinth. He passed through it all without finding her. He failed.

He's alone on the beach, only her voice drifting across to him, urging him back inside to find her. And he knows he has to. He pushes back the door to wander into the trap and sees her figure loom up deep inside the maze. She stands there waiting for him, dressed all in black, a light song on her lips.

"Poe!"

He opened his eyes to find Madigan standing over him, shaking him by the shoulders. "Snap out of it, man. We were beginning to lose you."

Poe straightened up in his chair. What had just happened? One moment he was thinking about Madigan's words, the next he's floating away, back into the past. "I remembered something. Being young. Something very strange."

Madigan released him and sat back down opposite. "If there's one thing I've learnt from studying the mind over the years, detective, it's that memory should never be trusted. Take Alan there," In the next room, another clone was cleaning up the last of the mess. "No memory at all to speak of. No childhood. Far more trustworthy, really."

Poe wasn't paying any attention. Something important had just happened. Something he'd just seen.

And then it clicked. A door opened. "Madigan. I saw her."

***

Gretchen. Not the most attractive name, even Adlai could admit that to himself, but it was her name, and that was all that mattered. She strode into the room and took charge immediately, weeding out the weak, organising those with skills she could use, bringing them close, becoming a leader by default. Adlai just sat back and watched her.

She was dangerous, he knew that immediately. Driven. She broke the rules whenever she could, bent the world around her to suit her needs. She was also beautiful.

There she was now, smiling as the chair in front of her raised itself into the air and began to spin, holding her arms out like a stage magician, green eyes glowing with power. The chair started to twist in on itself, lose shape. In moments it was just a mass of metal and wood, a ball of junk that thudded to the floor.

The room sank into silence, broken only when Adlai began a slow, lazy clap. "Bravo."

Her eyes flashed onto him then, freezing his hands. "You mock me?"

"No, no. I don't 'mock' you. I mock this." He gestured around the room, aware now that every eye was on him. "This conspiracy of ours. Of yours."

"You wish to leave? Leave then, we can do without the likes of you."

"And what is it you plan to do? Break down the walls with a barrage of broken chairs?"

"We will do whatever is necessary to regain the power we deserve."

Adlai let that statement hang in the air and looked around him. Driven indeed. "Nuts" might be another word for it. What was the point of VR if you lost all touch with reality itself?

As the silence stretched, heads turned back to their work, their games. Gretchen resumed her demonstration. Others did likewise, with various levels of success. Across the aisle the short, greasy man chuckled to himself and stood up. "You've made yourself an enemy there, I think. A powerful one. Not as powerful as some, perhaps, but powerful, nonetheless. This could be fun."

He shuffled away then, still chuckling into his chest. Adlai watched him go and then turned his head back to the various demonstrations. He wondered how many of them had real power.

Users were always trying to side-step the rules, but that was to be expected. It was half the fun, foiling their attempts. You were dealing with a part of the general population who were somewhat predisposed to cheating, to writing themselves shortcuts, to seeing themselves as outside the norm. You just had to be better than they were.

It occurred to him then that perhaps some of the mistakes around him were simple misdirection. To be truly effective, you honed your weapons in secret, you maintained the element of surprise. There were more dangerous weapons out there than these games. Weapons to alter the shape of reality itself, tools to take control of the environment, even other users.

Adlai went back to watching her. His eyes enjoyed trailing along her figure, memorising every line.

He waited until the bartender turned away before lifting his hand and watching the brown liquid in his glass rise up and wrap itself around it. A moment later he twitched his fingers and the liquid slowly poured itself back into his glass.

He took another sip. Always be sure not to affect the taste.

The miraculous was only interesting if it was hard to do. He didn't need to impress anyone. It was the same reason God had never turned up in church when he was younger. You shouldn't expect him to. He's not there to entertain you.

Which led to the question that always popped up after ten or so bourbons. What was he there for?

To bear witness perhaps. To look out the window and dream a new reality. To sit here on the fence, the border between two worlds. To watch what he'd done and suffer the consequences.

And now and then something came up that deserved his attention. His intervention. One was on its way now; he could feel the pull.

That was okay. He'd been waiting long enough.

***

Cass had heard stories about it around the office. Fellow workers had ventured out, explored the darker corners, went wandering away into the areas off-Grid. Made excuses to do it on company time or simply headed out and damned the consequences, safe in the knowledge their bosses knew less than was good for them.

They had the top hardware, that meant they should be able to handle whatever the outside world threw up at them, right? Cass smiled to herself at the thought. It was the usual company blind spot. Hardware is just a vehicle, an environment, what's important is what is running on it, the software, and how far it is able to bend the rules.

There had been a few casualties. Eyes staring out of windows in meetings, off into other universes where something important was left behind. Haunted, drawn faces who answered distractedly and stared down at their feet. She knew. She'd been living that life since the accident, since the nightmares. She figured nothing the River threw up could out-do reality.

The River for Cass had begun as a place to hide from reality, to forget, to dream in peace. She spent her time on Grid, wandering the same brightly lit streets, lazing on impossibly beautiful beaches, indulging in unlikely fantasy. It was safe and warm and never quite enough. It gave her happiness, at least the semblance of it, from the moment she lay down her head till the time her alarm screamed her awake but did nothing for the hours spent stuck in reality. The nightmares came back then, scratching at the backs of her eyes, waiting for a distracted moment to tear back into her.

The ones who ventured off-Grid, something stayed with them. You could see it. If something out there screwed with them that much it had to be worth trying.

Making her mind up was easy, the hard part was actually doing it. It wasn't just a matter of deciding to go off-Grid. The corporations didn't let you out that easily. They knew what was most likely to happen out there. It wasn't safe. They wanted their users to return, again and again. The only solution was to lock them in for their own protection. The walls around the Grid weren't just there to keep the monsters out.

There were some subversives. Scrawled graffiti on walls if you knew where to look. "Free the dreamers. Free the dreams." It never lasted long.

Cass had some advantages. She knew a few things, could try some tricks. None of it worked. Eventually she even resorted to asking other users for help. Most just smiled and walked away. The few who understood what it was she was asking for, they didn't bother with the smile.

Of course, when the answer came it was all too simple. Cass saw a user, older, slower, or perhaps he just chose to take his time, wandering down the centre of the street, staring at his feet. Head down, not bothering with the bright lights around him, a slight grin on his face. When she approached, he simply raised his hand and pointed down the middle of the road.

Cass's shoulders slumped and she was about to turn away when an amazing thing happened. She heard him speak.

"Always remember that the River is not on the Grid, it is the Grid which lies on the River."

She'd stared at him in numb shock. There was no way she should hear him, not here. He'd simply smiled and walked into her, through her, somehow disappearing before he got to the other side.

Cass was used to amazement, this place was awash with it. But this was the first time she'd actually been surprised.

***

Poe reached into his coat, brought out his notepad and started jotting down ideas as they came. The woman. The fear. The song. They were all linked somehow, and they all had something to do with the crash that had brought him out here in the first place.

"That's rather old fashioned, isn't it, detective?"

Madigan was peering at him with a curious smile on his face.

"It helps me keep my thoughts in order."

"Oh, I understand. I'm constantly forgetting things myself. I find it much easier that way."

Poe glanced up at him but didn't pocket the notebook. It was coming. Perhaps Madigan himself was the one to bring it on.

"Memory should never be trusted. We all effect our own interpretation of things – 'Wipe your glasses with what you know'. Alan and his brothers – clones, I suppose you'd call them – they don't need to worry about memory and its tricks. There are times I've thought about doing away with it completely.

"That song, for instance. I'd like to forget that. I know I won't. It was designed that way, designed to creep into your head and burrow around. The best you can do is bury it under other thoughts, try not to let it take hold and sprout. I've seen similar things before. Viruses. Designed to spread from mind to mind, worm their way in and overload the system. I helped build the first."

Madigan let his head drop and rubbed the lids of his eyes. He suddenly looked much older. "I'm constantly confused by my past actions, Detective. Perhaps that's just what age does. Someone once stated that the function of the mind is eliminative, not productive, that we have minds in order to help shut out the noise of the world, all the universes of information that we do not need. The overproduction of truth that cannot be consumed. Alan there, he doesn't need to worry about any of it. His mind functions clearly and sharply, no emotion allowed to get in the way. No memory to smudge. I think he could teach us a lot about what it means to think."

Poe flipped his notebook closed and pocketed it. This was what he had come for. "You said you've seen this before. Where?"

Madigan raised his head, and something like a smile came back to his lips. "Where? Why, right here of course. The great wonder that is the world off-Grid. You've seen it too, you know, at least a part of you has. That feeling you get when you hear it play, detective, that instinct that makes you cover your ears and huddle up like a child, that terror, that dread. The inevitability of fate, detective, we all recognise it. Some more that others, perhaps."

Poe waited. It would come.

"I think you should see a friend of mine, detective. A very old friend. Expert in the music field. She'll be able to tell you much more about this... problem."

Madigan held out a card to him but flipped it back into his palm as Poe reached for it. "Of course, I would expect my little operation here to remain off any official reports you feel you need to make."

Poe looked back into those calculating eyes that seemed to see so much and merely nodded.

"Very well then." The card flicked back out into Poe's hand and Madigan spun away. "I'd come with you, but you know how it is. So much to do, so little time."

A chuckle rose from Madigan's back. Poe reached out and took the memory stick from the top of the console.

"Besides, the streets are far too dangerous for a man of my age. Watch out for yourself, detective, there are those who won't be subdued by that gun you carry."

Madigan flicked a switch and a door appeared in the wall and swung open to reveal a dark, wet alley.

Poe walked out and turned around to face him. "Thank you."

"Godspeed, detective." Madigan flashed another grin and swung the door closed on the world.

***

Whenever he began to feel like this, this dread rising up in him, the knowledge of what it was he knew he was going to have to do, the guilt, Adlai found it best to head off on his own and take a long walk.

This street was perfect for it. One long strip, you could keep your head down and stare at your feet as the thoughts raced through you, and when they became too much you could look up at any time, at any one of the endless fascinations lining the banks, ready to distract you.

And the users themselves, wandering around with their heads in the air, new ones every day, lost among the endless possibility, they could help cheer him up. He knew why he was going to do it; he knew who for. And besides, company always helped.

He used to scrawl graffiti on the walls, simple messages to guide those with the curiosity to make the most of this world by themselves. This though, this would be much more direct.

The first step is always the most difficult. For Adlai this had been especially true. In order to build a universe, you need to make basic decisions. All of them. Not making a decision is itself a decision and affects all the others just as strongly. Everything needed to be defined, understood, and only then coded in.

He wasn't sure how he'd ended up in charge. He wasn't the brightest or best of them, perhaps just the most driven. He enjoyed exploring the consequences. Take the speed of light – was this still the upper limit here? The universe's traffic cop? If not, what other rules of physics would need to be tweaked? It wasn't easy.

In the end he made the only decision he could have – he kept things as close to reality as possible. Break too many laws, make your playground too different from the reality it's supposed to replace and you lose the entire point of VR. And then when other users come on board, make sure they follow the same rules, no matter what they want to try.

But what about later when the tools themselves become the problem? When the power and skills of the users become too great to limit, what then? Is there a limit to computational power, or will they just get faster and faster? Can you have processors running faster than the human brain, faster than the user will ever be able to appreciate? Computers that evolve beyond the understanding of humans, let alone their control? The Grid made the answer to that question pretty clear.

So, what were the consequences? The ultimate in VR was always directly inside the user's head, whether they were ported in or sleeping in a field. It altered their thoughts directly, creating in essence a different person altogether. So when the power became too great, could it run completely out of control?

Descartes had put that idea forward centuries before. There was a demon in our heads, manipulating our senses to trick us into believing the reality that surrounds us.

It was too easy to paint the Grid with that brush. Everyone needs a bad guy. Maybe that was its entire reason for being. A faceless evil, something to struggle against. Even God needs the Devil.

Adlai raised his head and looked up towards the towers, only to stop when he saw a lone female standing directly in front of him, the hunger of curiosity positively burning out of her. This was why he had to do it. This existence, this possibility could only take off when they stopped meddling in its universe, when all of them were free.

He knew exactly what she was looking for, it was the same thing he'd felt tugging at him from the beginning of all of this. He pointed down the centre of the River and whispered in her ear.

Adlai no longer remembered what it was he'd said, but he remembered the surprise on her face. He still saw them sometimes, those beautiful eyes glinting back at him from the bottom of his glass.

***

Cass waited and watched the lone man wandering down the centre of the street, rain bouncing off the brim of his hat. She sent out her senses, but they came back blank, just as they had before. He was a shell, nothing burning inside of him. No ghost in the machine.

He seemed harmless enough.

He had something though. It wasn't easy to stop a hunter like he had, leave it stunned in the street, flat on its back staring open eyed at the rain. Cass had found it still twitching and allowed her blade to finish the job. Not everyone could kill a hunter, especially one of the Brotherhood. They were quick and hungry, not to be taken lightly.

So, neither was he. Let the man pass, watch and wait.

She watched him stride past, head down, mouth moving as he chattered away to himself. She tried to sense what it was he said but it was hopeless. He wasn't projecting it out there for anyone to hear.

One stride later he stopped and peered into the darkness of her alley, directly at her. Cass tensed, ready to spring up the walls and away. The next moment, however, he turned away again and resumed his walk.

He had the sense, maybe not as tuned as Cass, but it was there. Instinct. Keep your distance.

The laneway was barely three feet wide, and as the lone man moved on Cass began to climb, pushing her arms out against each wall to brace herself, scampering up the storeys till she reached the rooftop, then curling her body over its edge to lie still, waiting for him. She couldn't place him with her senses. He was smudged out, coloured over with the usual hum from the outside world.

There he was, still wandering down the centre of the street. No traffic to worry about out here.

He had to be a cop. Someone from inside the Grid sent out to investigate the crash. She'd heard rumours of them. Quarters had told her about them in hushed tones, silent, dangerous enemies. No signature, no readable identity, no purpose. Tools of the Grid.

They were used to mop up problems before they reached the Grid itself. Take someone out, put something down. Even the hunters avoided them. But they usually came in packs, at least, so she'd been told. Always with a partner, never alone.

Cass sprung to her feet and padded silently across the rooftop, hardly making contact with the tiled surface as she sprinted across it. A leap and she was on the next rooftop, leaning back against the chimney stack, waiting for the man to walk back across her field of vision.

So why was he alone? Was that why the hunters hadn't recognised him, hadn't given him the wide berth they normally would have? Or were they not after him at all?

Who was using whom as the bait?

Cass looked down and found the blade in her hand again. It was hungry, it was always hungry now. She could feel it in her guts. What did it matter who the prey was? A turn of the wrist and she gazed at the letters stencilled into the base of its handle. That was why she was here, that was what she had to find. Madigan's. The clone had said they were expecting her.

She wrenched herself away from the figure and padded silently back in the direction he'd come from. She could feel her destination, she didn't need him to lead her there.

Her heart was pumping, not from exertion, but from something more. Excitement, but not from a kill. There was no aluminium tinge of blood and guilt, no feeling of loss of control. This was different. This was why she was here; this was her goal. She had found her purpose.

***

Poe remembered her. That figure in his nightmare, the woman in the maze, he'd encountered her before. Not exactly seen her but felt her presence. In that broken room with the first suffering victim he'd been led to. She had been there, a part of her at least. She was there in the memory card too, there in his pocket, there in the song that ripped out of it destroying all who heard it.

Even that clone had suffered. Anything with a thought in its head was a potential victim of the woman and the song.

"We're getting closer, Adlai. Connections are being made."

Poe walked slowly down the middle of the street, resolutely ignoring the ever-present rain that drummed on his hat. His hands were clasped behind his back, pushing him onwards, urging his brain deeper. The answer was somewhere up ahead.

Another clatter in an alley off to the side. Poe paused and turned to face the darkness of the alley curving away. There was something there, something best left alone. He turned away again and continued on.

"I'm too curious to be frightened, and too occupied to be curious. The dark corners have no power over us, son."

"Where are we going, exactly?"

Poe reached into his coat and read from the card Madigan had handed him. "'Wired for sound. When you require harmonisation'. It's not far from here. Nothing's ever far out here. Everything huddles together for warmth."

There were footsteps on the rooftop above and behind them.

"Don't look around, my boy, just keep walking. What was it Madigan said about the streets?"

"That they're dangerous."

"Yes, yes, but we already knew that. No, something else he said. Not about the streets, about the mind, the streets of the mind, all curving into each other, leading where?"

"The function of the mind is eliminative."

"Yes, that's it. Eliminative. We need them to filter out the noise. Noise like those footsteps perhaps. You can become distracted, start imagining things, creating images in your mind about possibilities, dark ones. Then you begin to tighten up, get the emotions involved, the adrenaline starts to flow, the muscles tense and you find yourself waiting for the sound of the next footstep. And somewhere deep inside, perhaps, a lullaby starts creeping around."

"So, we should ignore it?"

"Completely, my boy. Whoever or whatever it is will make itself known when it wants too. In the meantime, we have better things to think about."

"Such as?"

"Such as harmonisation. A fine word. A very musical word, really. Suggestions of tension, like a guitar string, or the dying breath of a flute. Focus, control. Like the mind, coiling into a tune. Interesting."

"I'm afraid you've lost me, sir."

"I'm afraid I've lost myself, lad, which when you think about it, is one and the same thing. No matter. These connections will become clear in time. Look. It seems we're here already. The power of the mind again you see."

They were on another anonymous dark lane, just like all the others. Dark, wet and unwelcoming. It never took long to find your goal out here, so long as it wanted to be found. The River always had a way of taking you right there.

Poe wasn't expecting another neon sign and didn't get it. Instead, there was a rain-streaked painted wall next to a small wooden door, a single button placed in it. Wired for sound. Above the door was a dull concrete insignia indented into the wall. The same three curved lines as before. He pressed the buzzer.

Nothing. The only sound was the constant percussion of the rain in the gutters.

"What now, sir?"

"Patience, my boy. Good things come, etc. There now, listen."

Above the rain another sound had been introduced, a series of small clicks, dancing along on top of the beat. Then, to round it all off, a creak as the door swung slowly open.

Poe waited, but nothing else happened and no one appeared. The room behind the door was a thick fog of darkness.

"Well now. After me."

He hunched his shoulders and walked inside.

*****

For Adlai it was about freedom, forcing the casual user back into being conscious of the possibilities of VR, back to taking responsibility for themselves. He didn't care what reasons the others claimed, they had a common enemy.

It didn't take long to narrow the group down to five, just those skilful enough to make a difference and desperate enough to try. They all had their own reasons for wanting to pull down the walls of the Grid.

Gretchen was the firebrand of the group, driven and passionate, she tried to take control at every opportunity. She was dangerous, which was exactly what was required. Adlai just had to stand back and watch her work, pushing the others onwards, squeezing every last drop of effort out of them.

And when threats and curses didn't work, she could turn on the charm to get her way. Adlai knew that firsthand. He wasn't immune, but he was wary. Ever since that first meeting when he'd challenged her, he'd seen the spark in the back of her eyes. She'd use whatever she could to take control of him.

The others weren't quite so dangerous, but they were just as useful. Madigan, the small greasy man he'd amused so much in the beginning, was a master with machines and materials, shaping and altering the world around him. He was producing their weapons, amazing things really. Adlai had watched them grow from simple blades to the reality altering wonders they were now.

Hound and Strafe, two expert hunters, masters of the war games so many of them still played to amuse themselves. Their job would be to run point, take care of any trouble they'd face forcing their way in. Each of the group had been their victim more than once out on the field. They were the best chance they had.

As for Adlai, he wasn't sure what he would do once he was in. There had to be a way to take down the Grid from the inside. If anyone could manage it, he supposed it had better be the one programmer most responsible for the River in the first place. That was as far as his plan went.

They really had no idea what they were doing. He could look back at that time now and almost smile. He was used to the guilt. What was that line about wearing it like an old suit? To Adlai it was more like a warm blanket he wrapped around himself, lifted over his head and burrowed into to keep the world out.

Fuck it. Have another drink.

It was hard keeping his mind in order. Alcohol helped cut down the options, helped stop his thoughts spiralling out of control. Like at night, when you close your eyes and relax and try to drift away and the whirlwind of past experience and future worry lifts you out of sleep and tosses you back and forth in your bed.

VR was part of the cure. It helped you switch off, both working on it and being in it. Like sitting in a church. Peaceful. That great emptiness surrounding you, the knowledge that you are a small part of a large whole. The stale air, the wooden pews and green leather kneeling pads. Maybe that's what he was trying to get back to.

And something more. Something hidden inside the chalice, behind the altar, in a shiny jewelled box that only the priest could open. Something awesome and out of this world. Something to be feared. Fear lived back there.

Fear and faith slept in the same place, wrapped in each other. Maybe to find one you first had to understand the other.

Part 3

The separation of dreamer from dream is demonstrated, our strange duo comes to recognise their unique potential, a living weapon fulfils its promise, and the inherent loneliness of technology's embrace is addressed.

Prologue

She was no longer completely sure that it had happened at all. Her dreams had moved in and altered the details, added touches and glimpses, shaded her memories a darker hue. It made no practical difference. All memories were altered with time, not just the ones you never managed to leave behind.

Thankfully, they never seeped through into her waking hours. Still, she could always tell when she'd had the nightmare. She'd wake with her head buried in the pillow, struggling to breathe, wet from sweat or tears or the River itself, a strange ringing in her ears as if they too remembered.

She was driving her sister's car down a long stretch of highway. Every few seconds her eyes would flick up and to the side, scanning the area for danger, glancing up at the two children in the back seat. Her nieces. They sat there turning pages in their books, idly singing a lullaby.

It was coming through the radio too, a simple tune. Familiar. In the dream she doesn't find it strange that such music pipes out. It's the second last thing her dreams ever allow her to hear.

The final one was only a second later. Looking back up from the radio to see a lone, pale figure standing in the middle of the road. Staring right through her. She wrenches the wheel to the side and the tyres scream in protest and whip the car sideways. That was the last sound she recognised, though she could never fully separate the scream of the eviscerating rubber from that of the girls in the back seat. The next moment a shockwave of water crashes over them, shattering the passenger side window, tearing red burns into the side of her face.

She had no scars, no physical scars, but they could heal, couldn't they? Not like the other ones, the ones that stayed within you.

Was it her dazed brain which slowed everything down, or her heightened reactions, the adrenaline pumping into her heart that made the next few moments shift past frame by frame? Unlock the belt, push open the door. Water rushing over her. Turning around to see the girls wrapped in each other, eyes staring in panic. A trickle of red running from her niece's ear. Water washing it away as it surged up and over their heads. An arm grabbing her, demanding she flee the wreck, not listening to her pull back, not allowing her to disentangle the children.

The sunlight warm through the water, then gone again the next instant as she pulled away and dived back down, only to be caught again and dragged out. Numbness. The world around her spinning, trying to catch back up to normal speed.

Sitting on the bank, staring at the calm surface of the river. Hands over her ears, not allowing any further sound in. No one else around her was wet – who had pulled her out? Maybe there had never been anyone else. Maybe it had just been her, deciding to save herself and let the girls drown. She could see the same thoughts reflected back at her from everyone's eyes.

Then much later, lying in bed. Her sister next to her, shaking her, screaming at her. Not being able to hear a thing. Some things are taken away from us for a reason.

Poe had somehow been expecting it, but it made him jump, nonetheless, when the door he'd just walked through slammed closed behind him and a series of locks clicked back into place.

Around him were matt grey walls, shadows moping in the corners, then wandering away as his eyes adjusted to the darkness. He took a step, then stopped as he noticed something missing.

There was no sound. Absolute silence. No rain drumming on the roof, no wind. He stamped his boot on the ground, but still could hear nothing. He clapped his hands. Nothing.

His brain jumped and started rushing down into panic, but he reined it back. Let curiosity take over. He could feel Adlai's words in his head, if no longer hear them.

Poe clapped again, this time letting his eyes soak in the details. The wall closest to him seemed to spark for a moment. He walked closer and ran his hand across it. It was spongy, almost wet, not natural. It felt like the inside of someone's throat.

"Hey!"

The shout brought a brief wash of colour to the wall before it faded. His ears had again heard nothing. It was as if the sound itself had leapt out of his mouth and become stuck inside the walls, caught like a fly and then spirited off. Detoured.

"Hello?"

It was a very strange feeling to talk and not hear oneself. Not even the usual muffled buzz from the inside when the sound can't reach you through your ears and seems to slice through the throat straight to the brain. Just utter silence roaring back.

"Hello? My name is Poe. Detective Poe."

He hoped what he was saying made sense. He couldn't tell if he was pronouncing his syllables correctly, couldn't judge himself and alter his tongue. "Madigan sent me."

At that a light appeared at the far end of the room. He immediately walked towards it and realised with a jerk that he could hear again as his boots clomped on the floor.

"Hello?" A foolish sense of relief rose up as he heard the word.

The light ahead became the frame of a door, and he slowly pushed it open to reveal the exact opposite of the room he'd just left.

Mess. Complete and utter visual pandemonium. Wires, cords, cables, speakers, microphones, metal stands, all seemingly thrown together in a heap and somehow landing right side up. Everything seemed to sweep up into a platform at the far end, and behind that was the top of someone's head, bouncing back and forth.

The walls were covered in speakers, some vibrating but no sound coming out. At least nothing he could hear. He could feel it though, feel the thickness in the air, the tingling of sound rushing across him, pushing him back up towards the raised platform, herding him in the right direction.

As he approached, the figure became clearer. At first he thought it was a child, but then realised he was staring at an extremely old woman. All four foot of her.

Almost a quarter of that seemed to be hair. She had a high bun piled on the top of her head, and it was this that was moving to the sound he couldn't hear.

Closer still and he could see she was sitting down, a long dress covering the chair underneath her, hands clasped to the chair's arms as she swept back and forth. There was something wrong with the proportions though. Her head was too big for her body, and no feet peeked out from the base of her dress, just empty air.

Poe tried not to stare, but then came to her eyes and couldn't help himself. They shone straight through him, as if a bright fire danced behind them, giggling at him, lighting him up and reading him at the same time. He recognised their similarity to Madigan's straight away, but there was something more. A dangerous glint.

He looked away as they held him and felt the sound waves around him die off. When it finally came, her voice was brittle and old, fitting everything but those dangerous eyes. "Been to see Madigan, have we? Waste your time, did he? Always does, always does."

Poe just stood and waited.

"Told him a million times. Stop messing about with those gadgets, those clones. Did enough damage already with those blades. Don't draw attention to yourself. People like us, knowing what we know, should keep our heads down. Never listens though, that man. Never did."

Her chair moved across the platform and came to rest in front of him. "Take me, for example. Look at me."

Poe felt his head snap up and stared at her.

"Been in this chair more years than anyone can remember. And for what? For not keeping my head down, that's what. Madigan knows. He got it too, had part of him taken away. Maybe it was the part that listens. Hmph."

The chair turned away again and a thin arm reached out from the folds of her dress to touch a button on the console in front of her. A light music swelled up from the floor and wrapped itself around them. Poe let out his breath.

"Have a seat, boy."

A chair rose from the cable strewn floor and took his weight.

"Now, let's get down to it."

Poe felt his body relax and sank down into helplessness as her eyes turned on him.

***

"Let me quote you something here…" What the fuck was his name again? Jack? "Barkeep." His words were beginning to slur. That was okay, it kept them in line with his thoughts.

"'The man of knowledge in our time is bowed down under a burden he never imagined he would ever have: the overproduction of truth that cannot be consumed.' What do you think of that? Know who wrote it? Ernest… Ernest somebody, long time ago. When he says 'our time' he's talking about something a lot different from ours. Mine."

Why didn't this bar ever change? Maybe he should look at altering something. Always the same amount of people, always the same light.

"It's bullshit, too, of course. I mean, I understand what he's trying to say. Back in the distant past, man's search was for truth. For meaning. Then we started to find answers and it all went to shit."

The window never changed. Same shape, same size, same darkness and rain. When he was younger, he used to make pictures in the clouds but all he saw were other people's faces.

"Too many answers then. So what do we do? We start making shit up. Fooling each other. Maybe we were trying to lighten that burden he was talking about. Stop worrying so much about truth, about meaning."

That wasn't true, Adlai had never given up that search. At least, not until he found himself here.

"I mean, when you think about it, what is there to really believe in anyway? Everything can be faked, and most of it is. The news is skewed, sliced and diced into comfortable sound bites; photographs, those little snapshots of the world people used to trust so much, remember them? All airbrushed, tweaked and clipped. Nothing sadder than an edited photo. What's the fucking point? The overproduction of truth. Bah."

His cigarette packet was empty but another, full one appeared a moment later by his right hand. He grabbed it and ripped it open.

"That's what people never understood. What's the difference between VR and reality now? You can do what you want, be what you want, and when you screw up, you face the consequences. No different at all. The River is just more honest."

Someone had asked him once why he thought it had to exist at all. What could it offer that the real world couldn't? He couldn't remember what his answer had been, or even if he'd had one. He had one now. The River was a playground where you learned how to live. Like the old view of life as a training ground for death, for the afterlife and the judgement yet to come.

"We managed to fuck it up though, didn't we. Always do. Can't trust kids not to break their toys. Lead a horse to water and all that. Speaking of."

He took another drink and resumed staring out at the rain, forming the shapes into fantasy. His hands were clutched together and he began rubbing his left ring finger, worrying something which had never been there.

***

Since the split Cass's life was a daze. She just drifted along, waiting for the next event to occur.

Wake up in the morning and stare at the ceiling, trying to dredge up the memories of the night before, the dreams that are no longer there. Get dressed in the same clothes you wear every Tuesday. Stand on the train surrounded by people dressed exactly the same, feeling the same way, doing the same thing. But still strangers.

She was jealous of the readers, those with heads stuck in books, somewhere else, lost among the worlds. She couldn't lose herself like that anymore. It had all been taken away.

Get to work, spend an hour churning through emails, an hour plugging code into the system, an hour reading the newspapers. Then lunch. Eat and lie in the park, in the foreign sun, and try to dream.

Afternoon meetings surrounded by people talking earnestly about the new hardware, about how many more users they could get online. People she would never understand. Did they actually care about this job? Didn't they just join up for the hardware, for the knowledge, for the possibilities?

Cass nodded her head and stared out the window, placing an expression of thought upon her face. Smiled when expected to.

Leave the office early, sneak out while no one's looking, catch the early train home, picking up food on the way. The same thing you eat every Tuesday. Eat early and quickly till a wave of tiredness washes over you. Retreat into bed and start looking again, hunting for the life you lost, the dreams you lost.

Cass knew she had to stop drifting like this, but what were the options? Find a new job? What possible difference would that make? They were all the same, the Corporations. As similar as their blocks on the Grid. You could change addresses, but you were always on the same street. The River didn't change.

Besides, at least she had access to the latest gear. If anyone was going to find what she was looking for, it was her. The entire back wall of her bedroom was a VR unit, state-of-the art, she no longer even needed to jack, simply lay back and let the field surround her, let the dreams take her away until she found herself back on the wet streets.

That was how it should be. Now she was simply wiped out by a dark fog, not remembering anything, no connection found. A black, dreamless sleep. An unsuccessful hunt.

She could go out after work and watch other people get along. Sit at the bar and wait for lonely men to approach, but it was unsatisfying, lightweight. They tried to sell her an image she disdained, of herself as well as them. And when something did happen, when you drank yourself into enough of a stupor for your heart to allow a connection, even then it ended quickly. Lie there in the dark and stare at the ceiling, waiting for him to finish, wait for sleep to take him away from you so you can stare at his face and wonder what the world looked like through that.

Introversion was overrated. You weren't supposed to find the answers on your own, you were supposed to socialise, mingle with each other, live through the reflections others glance back off of you. That's what VR was for, that's what the River had been all about. All she could do was keep looking.

She knew this, so she tried to toe the line, waiting for her dreams to come back into focus and take her away.

***

Adlai let the glass slip back from his lips and rest on the bar. A few drops had spilt onto its dull wooden surface. He traced circles idly through them.

He missed her, he could admit that now. At least, he missed his memory of her back in the beginning. Maybe he was wrong, maybe he just missed company. An audience.

Sometimes he wondered to himself, had she really happened? Could he be sure she wasn't another in a long line of fantasies dreamt up and then created to immerse himself in? How many of his dreams were out there running around now? Such thoughts used to trouble him.

No, she was real enough. He may have turned her into what she was now, but she was real, nevertheless.

He remembered the exact point when it started to go sour. They'd been in another meeting, arguing amongst themselves, taking two steps back for every three forward. They were all reaching breaking point. Gretchen had finally leant over and whispered to him that she wanted to show him something, something the others weren't yet ready to see, and he knew straight away she was trying to trap him.

He couldn't really blame her, much as you couldn't blame a wild animal from striking out at you. It was her nature; he'd seen it from the beginning. He nodded his head and got back to what the group was talking about, but that was the moment. He remembered the stillness of it, the feeling of the world shifting around him. It wasn't shock, or sadness, but something else. A revelation.

"Nothing wrong with it, is there?" He fished a cigarette out and tried to ignore his shaking hands. "That's why we have this place. William James."

Finally, it caught and he sucked back smoke.

"William James said that mankind held the world to be essentially a theatre for heroism. Nice idea. Not sure about the heroism part, but theatre? Bang on the money. Make believe. We all fool ourselves, and we all want an audience."

Maybe that's why he'd let himself be drawn in. Certainly, it was why he kept going, well past the point where he should have turned his back and walked away. He was drowning in loneliness. He was willing to cling on to whoever drifted past.

"Not anymore though." Adlai downed the last of the drink and let out a long, tired breath. "Not anymore."

He sat and stared and only let go of the glass when a full one stood next to it.

***

"Name?"

"Edgar Poe."

He didn't even think, couldn't think. The words simply blurted out of him.

"You don't say. Someone has a sense of humour. Business?"

"Detective. Investigating a death off-Grid."

"Murder most foul and all that, hmm? And what has led you here, detective?"

"This."

He looked down and the memory stick was in his outstretched palm.

Her eyes seemed to spark a little brighter as she looked down on it, and she reached out and touched a button on the arm of her chair. The music released its grip and Poe felt his mind clear.

"I would apologise, detective, but I find it unnecessary. This saves a lot of time, though some find it unpleasant. Saving time becomes important when you get to my age."

The voice which just a moment ago had been so eager to leap out of him seemed to have disappeared back down inside. He sat and stared.

"Here." She whirred her way across the room to him holding out a glass of water. "Drink, it will help."

Her eyes seemed kinder somehow, dimmer. Younger.

Poe drank and felt his throat loosen. "What was that?"

"The music? It is my gift, detective, my power. My weapon."

Poe continued to drink. He hadn't realised how thirsty he was.

"It can leave you dry and weak afterwards. Poor detective."

There was a glint to her smile now as she waited. Eventually Poe downed the glass and took control.

"What is your name?"

"Of course, how rude of me. Madigan wouldn't have wanted to spoil the surprise, not him."

She turned her chair and slid away again, moving back and forth to some hidden beat.

"My name. I've gone by many over the years. Which one would you recognise? Gretchen perhaps."

"Gretchen?"

"Or perhaps not. Seems I've been keeping my head down more than I thought, hmm? No matter."

Her movements were jerkier, quicker now. Angry, perhaps? Poe wondered if she was as easy to read as that. "What can you tell me about the music on this memory card? Madigan sent me to you because he thought you'd know more."

"No doubting that, child. It's whether what I know is worth telling you. Whether you can make it worth my while."

There was another buzz in the air, and Poe felt the constriction around his throat. "What is that noise?"

"Noise, detective? I hear nothing." She was grinning at him again, relishing her display of power.

"Stop it!" Poe felt himself stand and the air around him cleared.

Gretchen ceased her swaying and stared at him.

"I see you do have some talent, detective. Not many men could shrug off even such a simple shackle alone."

She continued to stare, and Poe had the uncomfortable feeling she could see more than he intended. Alone?

A moment later she turned again, and the tension dropped. "Here, detective, as a gesture of truce, I'll show you."

She motioned him over to the control panel in front of her and pointed to a small dial. "A simple emotional control. This dial primes the speakers that surround you, causing the air particles to vibrate. This vibration ends up in your inner ear, which is why you hear that buzz. It electrifies the air around you, putting your emotions on edge, ready to be guided one way or the other. Very effective on those with less self-control. Not so on you, hmm?"

The dial had numbers all around it. Poe doubted he'd felt more than a shade of its possibilities.

"Oh yes, detective. It can do much more than make you tell the truth. But that's not what I want from you."

Now they were getting to it.

"There are times even old travellers like myself need a little help from those like you, detective, those who patrol the River, keeping it straight, or at least, clean."

Poe opened his mouth to speak but Gretchen waved him away. "You, detective, are here to find out about whatever is inside that memory stick of yours which seems to do so much damage when let out. I am here to learn a little about you along the way. We can help each other, hmm? Sit."

A chair had risen underneath him again. Whatever this room was, underneath its veined, cabled skin was something almost living.

The thought flashed across him – how did she know what was on the card?

"Perhaps we should start with something simple."

Gretchen reached out and took the memory card from his hand and placed it delicately on the control panel. "Tell me, detective, what do you know about sound?"

***

Cass couldn't be sure how much time had passed when she found herself staring at the familiar symbol on a flickering neon sign outside a dirty, blank wall. Time had a way of warping, wrapping and twisting its way around the River. Some moments seemed to last forever, others flashed past like a knife to the throat.

The building looked old and run down, but Cass knew better than to trust first impressions. You didn't survive out here without secrets.

She flipped down onto the street floor and crept up to the wall. It tingled under her fingers as she leant against it, brushing her hands across its surface. There was power here.

As her hand passed over it a small panel slid open in the blank expanse and a monitor appeared, showing an old man's face smiling out at her. Cass stepped back and to the side quickly, but then paused. There was no danger yet.

The eyes on the screen followed her. "Hello there! A visitor, and a distinguished one at that, Alan. Your namesake has produced as always!"

The voice poured out of the speaker with complete clarity, aiming itself straight for her, entering her mind and speaking louder than any ear could hear.

"Cass, is it not? Your reputation precedes you. You'll excuse me if I don't meet you in person, of course, it's just that I don't want to add to it."

The voice was old, sing-song. It belied the power Cass could see burning out from behind his eyes.

"It's been quite the day for visitors. Someone's been stirring the pot, bringing everything back up to the surface, hmm? No, I think we'll stay tucked away in here for the time being, Alan. Far safer than what roams those streets."

The eyes grinned at her, waiting for some kind of response. Wait. Wait and watch and be ready to spring.

"Oh, my apologies, this voice and in particular, the fact that you can hear it may come as some surprise. Please, do not be alarmed. I've learnt a few tricks in my time out here. Believe me, it is by no means the limit of my talents."

As he spoke the walls around the monitor began to warp and sink backwards, stretching themselves out and then reaching back and around her. As Cass tensed to spring they pulled away again, bending out from her and opening to reveal a simple white room containing a single figure.

"Excuse me, one cannot resist a little showmanship now and then. You need to flex the muscles to keep them in shape, though I'm sure I don't need to tell you that. Pleased to meet you, my name is Madigan."

Cass stared down at the proffered hand until it slunk back behind his back. Then she let her eyes scan back up to his face. There was something missing there. A glance down at her side revealed that the blade was already in her hand.

The clone backed away, holding up its hands now, a blank smile on its face. "Now, now, young lady, there's no need for any further display of your prowess. I'm quite aware of what you can do. There's no threat here, simply an old man and his games. Madigan, of course, isn't here right now, but please be assured that I speak directly for him. My name is Alan. I believe we've met."

Cass felt the tightening at the base of her spine relax and come back under control, the blood lust sink back down into her gut. She flipped the blade around and held it up to the clone's face, handle first. She watched his eyes take in the small insignia marked on its base.

"Ah, yes, I was wondering when I'd see one of these again."

***

"Do you think God's ever disappointed with himself?" Adlai asked.

The bartender continued to ignore him. That was okay, he wasn't expecting an answer.

A work of art never turns out quite as you expect, but you can usually guarantee you'll be disappointed. That's not to say it wasn't worth creating in the first place, just that your goal wasn't fully realised. It's not quite the way you wanted it to be.

This, the River, was like that. Where some saw a fascinatingly deep universe filled with dark corners to disappear into, bright lights to dazzle and distract, Adlai saw a lost opportunity. It was very far from what he'd intended.

The frustrating thing was he no longer even remembered what it was he had been trying to do, what he'd aimed for. He just knew he'd missed.

There were glimpses. A place where users would plug in and confront their dreams, confront possibility and begin to understand the nature of their own lives. A place to explore what it was to be human. A church in which to confront God.

Now? Now it was a playground.

He knew it while he was sitting in their little meetings, being drawn along by their enthusiasm, knew it while he was letting his eyes wander over Gretchen, letting her dig her claws into him. He knew it especially when he wandered down the River alone, watching the users fumble about in their new world. It had to end. The question was what was worth saving.

A large part of being human, of consciousness, is not understanding what drives you. You float along on top of a tide of unconsciousness, hidden agendas and desires that push and pull you in different directions, directions you never had any intention of heading in, directions you never even knew existed. Possibility.

Trying to whittle it all down to the essence of what life was all about was destined to be unsuccessful, disappointing. Not what you intended. Still, that didn't mean it wasn't worth doing. After all, maybe someone else, some stranger you drifted into on the River one night, maybe they could stumble into their own answers. Your job was to allow them that chance.

Adlai motioned to the bartender and flicked through some code. "Let's hear it one more time."

The bartender stood directly in front of him. His eyes lost focus as the old programme was run through him once again.

"Art exists that one may recover the sensation of life; it exists to make one feel things, to make the stone stony. The purpose of art is to impart the sensation of things as they are perceived and not as they are known."

Two steps to the left and he was back in his usual place, unaware of what had just passed through him.

Was that what had become of this place for Adlai, was it just another reflection of what his work might have been? Another failure?

Adlai took up his glass again and let his mind drift away.

***

Poe sat still in his chair and waited for her. Sometimes the best form of questioning is to simply allow them to say what they want.

"Sound, detective, the vibration of air particles in the ear, a direct connection to the emotional centres in the brain, altering the way you experience the world. Your inner ear detects the sound and you respond psychologically, hmm? That is music's goal, to play off this power, to rouse the emotions, to release or relieve them, to stimulate the listener. Music is not just sound mathematics; it is the most powerful of all art forms because it speaks to a part of your being you can never directly access yourself – your emotions."

Poe could feel the questions inside him but let them pass. Wait and the answers will come.

"Too often these emotions are wrapped up in thought, feeding back into each other, muddying up the waters of your mind. Music skips along the surface like a stone, creating ripples, and then sinking down into the intellect. It is the reverse of poetry, it begins by activating feelings, then moves onto thought. That is its point, its power and its weakness, hmm? It relies on the listener's own imagination."

The familiar tune, the childhood nightmare. They were all part of him. Just like Adlai.

"Because of this it can be immensely powerful. It can hypnotise, soothe the savage beast, control and contort the listener. Let me ask you, detective, when you hear a tune in the minor key, a mournful tune, do you feel sad? Is this emotion wrapped up in the music itself, or does it only reside in you? Is it possible for you to recognise a song as sad without feeling sad yourself? What about anger, hmm? What if a song can access other emotions? Larger, more dangerous ones, ones that consume you, like fear. What if it can then hitch a ride in and break your mind down completely?"

She knows all about the card already. The song, the victims, the creeping fear that still tried to poke its head up from the surface. That he had to still concentrate to keep submerged lest the tune swirl about him again, become a whirlpool that sucked him down and away.

"It's a virus. A weapon." He could feel himself sweating but clenched his fist and forced himself to calm.

Gretchen smiled. "You catch on quickly, detective."

"But why would someone create something like this, something so dangerous?"

"Powerful is the word we used."

He heard the truth in the words as soon as they were uttered. "You did this."

"Let's just say it was my idea. Others had a hand in its design, and I imagine it has altered itself considerably since then. One must adapt to survive."

Gretchen swivelled in her chair and touched the control panel in front of her. The memory card still sat alone on the desk. Neither of them wanted to touch it. "You must understand, detective, we were idealists. We had an honourable goal in mind. One makes a lot of mistakes when young, hmm? Not all of them come back to haunt you."

Light music began to fill the room again, and Poe knew he was helpless. He had been since he walked in the door.

"We were angry. Angry and clever and young, and that is a dangerous cocktail."

She glanced back at him and saw the tension in his face. "Relax, detective, not all weapons are evil. Sometimes it is easier to show than tell."

He relaxed; he was powerless not to.

Poe felt himself sink down into his chair as the room seemed to fill with light. Soon it was too bright for his eyes. He closed them and another world appeared.

Daylight. The word ran into his head from the past, from somewhere he'd forgotten. The sun. Clear blue skies. Altogether alien to him, yet suddenly familiar. He looked down at the sun warming the bare skin of his arm. How could he have forgotten this? What was this place?

"This, detective, is the world as it was."

***

Cass started as a door suddenly appeared in the far wall and the same old man walked into the room. The same, but different. Whole. "You may leave us now, Alan, thank you."

The clone smiled and nodded to Cass before turning and leaving through the door which then vanished into a blank white wall.

"You will excuse us, of course. As I mentioned, one cannot be too careful in these parts, especially these days. Madigan is my name."

Cass studied the old man and immediately felt the life and power radiating out of him. This was no clone. There was a depth, a mass she could feel slightly warping the world around him, bending it with his presence.

"Oh, yes, I am the real thing. I should have known you'd pick up on Alan immediately, but one does enjoy one's little tests. You did much better than my earlier visitor, though you do have quite distinct talents."

His bright eyes drifted down to the blade still clasped in her hand. "May I see it?"

The only thing to trust was instinct, and it told Cass to trust this man. She handed the blade over.

As it left her hand she felt a deep pull in her gut, a tearing, a yearning to have it back. Her shoulders tensed but she controlled the urge to spring.

"It's been quite some time since I held one of these. There are others, of course, not all the same shape or size or power, but all capable of some surprising results. I assume you know?"

Madigan stepped over to the wall and dug the blade into it. He sliced it down effortlessly. "Yes. Perhaps a little too powerful if I do say so myself."

He tossed the blade back to Cass quickly, and she caught it by the hilt and slung it onto her waist. It was still warm from his hand.

"I called them Rippers. Designed to alter the fabric of reality, at least, what we on this side consider reality to be. They were made for a specific purpose, long ago. Made by me. One of my most successful creations. Successful and dangerous. Now they've gone the way of all forgotten things here and become altered. Scattered. Their name changed, now they call them River Blades. Yet the power still remains and with that the danger."

He wiped his hand down his gown as if eager to lose the sense of the blade against his skin. "They have other names. Blood Drinkers. Warpers. Twisters. One of their unfortunate side effects, I'm afraid. They tend to alter the wielder slightly with each use, warp them as they warp reality. Create hunger and chaos. You should be careful, it's already quite advanced with you."

Cass felt a sudden urge to grab the blade again, but she suppressed it. Wait. He is leading you somewhere.

"They have a way of finding those who were meant to wield them. It seems to have found you well enough. Perhaps it knows its purpose better than I. My creations often surprise me. Take Alan here for instance."

Immediately, the door reappeared and another clone walked in.

"Alan, what was that song I heard you all singing the other day?"

The clone smiled shyly and lifted his head.

"Row, row, row your boat

Gently down the stream.

Merrily, merrily, merrily, merrily

Life is but a dream."

Madigan clapped his hands together. "Bravo!" He looked at Cass. "I never taught them that, lord knows who did."

He grinned to himself and shook his head. "Quite apt really. As I said, constantly surprising. Thank you again, Alan, that will be all."

The clone smiled happily and turned to leave.

"Oh, just one more thing."

Madigan stepped quickly in front of the clone and out the door before him. A moment later the door was gone, leaving Cass and the clone staring at the wall.

Cass felt her hand tighten.

"Sorry about this, old boy, it's just that I've learnt to read certain people, especially those addicted to something I've created."

The voice was echoing from the roof now. Cass looked down and found the blade ready in her hand.

"Our friend here should prove quite useful, but unfortunately, she's also a little hard to control at the moment. She is a weapon herself, now. A true River Blade. Best to keep at arm's length."

Alan turned towards her and smiled hopefully. She saw a dark shadow reflected in his empty eyes.

Cass sprung back against the wall then up and over the unmoving figure. She flipped and landed lightly behind him, reached around his head, and in one movement twisted his neck and let the blade bite hungrily into his throat.

There was no blood, just a slumped figure on the floor. Cass felt herself relax and was surprised when she found herself breathing again.

The voice echoed down from the roof.

"Such a pity."

***

Poe stood silent, dazzled by the sun. Standing next to him was Gretchen, but not Gretchen. She was young, mid-twenties, a vibrant energy coursing through her. Curly copper hair stringing down over her shoulders, set off against the bright green eyes that sniped out at you from under her fringe.

"Time never means much on this side, but even so, this was long ago. Look."

Poe reluctantly let his eyes slip from her face and follow her hand to a point on the horizon. He stared uncomprehending before he realised what was wrong. Something was missing. The Grid.

Where there should be towers of bright steel, glowing with power and energy, shining out against the darkness, there was simply empty space. He looked harder and the area morphed into a white sandy beach, then a moment later into a verdant forest. It kept on shifting, turning and glinting in the sun.

"This is how we began. Creators in our very own playground, providing visions and experiences for all. What is for you a forest is for someone else a mountain, for others still a desert. There is no definitive. As time passes, our areas grow."

Poe stared as the world seemed to explode outwards in all directions at once, making connections, feeding itself, growing like a fungus. Definitively alive.

"There are those, however, who are never comfortable with freedom without control. These people took a foothold in the universe and built what is now known as the Grid."

The view seemed to shoot back in again, zoom to a level where details were clear. A pair of golden towers were beginning to rise, and a straight strip of darkness edged its way across the horizon.

"At first, we ignored it. Snickered. This was merely a corporate block in the playground for those not strong enough, or brave enough, to weather life outside without a parent. It was unsurprising. Let them have their slice of the River. Let them have their Grid."

More towers sprouted, glowing with energy now. The surrounding areas seemed to fade by comparison.

"It wasn't long before we became aware of the true effects. Power is not infinite. For someone to become stronger, another must weaken. As the Grid began to glow, other nodes became dark. By the time those of us who had any real power noticed, it was too late to stop."

The sky around them darkened, and a steady rain began to pour. From far above they looked down, and all Poe could make out were various angry bright flashes on the edge of the Grid. Red splotches of light flaring up and quickly darkening as they were overwhelmed.

"Many tried, of course, but one of the main weaknesses of ultimate freedom is the lack of organization, lack of unity. Even then, if we had found a leader willing to stand up, willing to work with us, focus our efforts, the Grid would never have withstood us. Unfortunately, that was not to be."

The Grid had grown a hundred-fold, swelled both in size and brightness, until it took on the shape Poe recognised. The off-Grid areas were dark now, the shady, wet streets that he knew. Hidden corners filled with danger.

"Then came our final mistake. Not content with mere fumblings, we planned a final assault. In it, we introduced a virus code, designed to break the fabric of the system down from the inside. We cannot see this from here. Come."

Immediately they zoomed into a point just off-Grid, a lonely twisting street, just another extension of the River.

"Watch."

A lone man walked along the centre of the laneway, head down as the rain dripped off the brim of his hat. Poe felt a shock of recognition and energy. It was him. And there was something else, a buzz in the air. The man raised his head and stared off into a dark alley. Poe knew what he saw.

There she stood. A dark-clad figure, hands clasped in front of her, standing erect and still. Eyes flashing back from under her fringe.

Poe tried to keep his eyes on her but couldn't, he dropped his head and held his ears, blocking out the song, which was not there but which played itself in his memory. He watched the figure close in and engulf the man, absorb him. Then she paused and turned towards him.

"Enough."

He opened his eyes and stared at the cables on the floor. They were back in Gretchen's control room. They were safe.

"Her power is too great."

She pushed her chair back and fiddled idly with some more controls on the panel in front of her. "We didn't understand what we were doing. It was all his fault, he drove us to it, just because he'd started it all in the first place. Now it's out of control. Only a matter of time, hmm? Time and melody."

Poe let his eyes scan across the room again, at the speakers lining the walls, the microphones hanging from every fixture. That's what this place was, a bunker. A hideaway. He looked up at Gretchen with fresh eyes. She was just a scared old woman. She couldn't help him anymore. Unless.

His intellect made the leap as the words left his mouth. "Who's 'he'?"

Gretchen stared back at him and a smile crept around the edges of her mouth. "Of course, you wouldn't know any longer, would you, detective? You were severed at the time, you all were. A catastrophe of epic proportions, now completely forgotten, at least on this side. Now the dreams are free, hmm? 'He' is the one who designed this universe. 'He' was the leader of our little group. 'He' is the one now missing, hiding away somewhere, watching his creation fade into darkness. 'He' is the one who stranded me here, forced me into hiding. 'He' is your father, detective, your dreamer, your connection to the other side. And you're going to help me find him."

***

Adlai walked slowly down the centre of the lane, staring at his shoes, letting the rain drip down from the brim of his hat. He enjoyed the rain. It had been someone else's idea to darken the areas off-Grid, make them less accessible to the casual user, less attractive. Perhaps it had come from the Grid itself, Adlai had never bothered himself to check. He found it comforting, almost romantic. It left him alone with his thoughts.

It would only be a matter of time before Gretchen or one of the others took their weapons and turned them on him. He knew that, expected it. He would have to be ready to act first. Besides, his work was greater than all of theirs combined. He knew what he planned would be seen as a betrayal. Perhaps in time it would be recognised for what it really was.

His thoughts turned back to the world around him, to the sound of his boots on the road, the rain on the rooftops. There was something else there, something new. He let his feet continue on and switched his awareness to searching it out.

There.

Very slight, almost not there at all. A humming. A female voice, lilting across a simple tune, repeating them over and over.

The air around him charged with danger. He stopped his walk and looked into the shadows, knowing what he would find there.

A single figure, a woman, dressed all in black, grim, pale face drawn tight around the lips. Adlai felt fear and panic course through him, up and down his spine, grabbing him by the back of the head and holding him still. She began to drift towards him.

Her body never moved, but she came closer. Watching him, a promise of misery in her eyes. Her green eyes.

Adlai snapped his eyes away from the figure and called out. "Gretchen!"

The fear and electricity around him melted away instantly. The figure vanished, as did the subtle tune that started it all. A moment later Gretchen finally made herself known, stepping out from the shadows of the lane, a small smile on her lips. "I thought you'd like it."

Looking back, she hadn't had to stop. Perhaps she was nervous, unsure whether it was quite ready to take him out. He wasn't sure either. It would have been a close-run thing.

Or perhaps it was all just a display, a flexing of her muscles, a reminder of what she could offer. You could never tell with Gretchen. Adlai doubted she even knew herself.

Her creation was a stroke of genius, you had to give her that. She was one of the cleverest of the programmers, one of the most promising. Was it wrong to think of them as disciples?

Adlai took another sip and let the liquid wash around between his teeth. He swallowed with a grimace and set the glass down. One benefit of being alone is that there's no one around to argue with you.

She'd designed the virus to enter the user's consciousness through music. Drift in and get stuck inside, through the ears, into the brain, a constant tune repeating itself, growing like a culture in a petri dish. Crawling up into the amygdala and squeezing. Linking into the user's fear centre, rendering them helpless. Hallucination feeding on hallucination until there was nothing left, until the users themselves were eaten away by fear and panic. It attacked the consciousness behind each dream, the hardware. Take that away and the dream itself dies, as sudden and sure as waking the dreamer.

The intention was to attack the Grid, attack the powers that fed it. Get in underneath the radar and infest the great quantum computers that ran the constructs. If it knocked out a few genuine users on the way, well, think of them as acceptable losses.

That's what Gretchen had claimed, anyway. Adlai had reservations about her motives, and besides, he saw much greater potential in it.

He was beginning to realise the limits he had imposed on the River. They had been necessary to begin with, but were they still? Was it time to begin practising what he preached?

A cell has to split to grow, only then can it go on to become what it needs to. An organism, a virus. Consciousness is not alive, it is a collection of life, an environment for it. A world of possibility.

Time would prove him right. Break the connection between the two worlds, force the dreams to realise themselves, force the users to face reality. They'd come to call it the Separation. He preferred the term emancipation, but perhaps that was asking too much. Just get it done and sit back and watch the show. Have a drink. What needed to go around would come around again.

Sooner or later everyone's dream would walk into the bar. Even your own.

***

"Feeling better now, are we?"

Cass let her breath rush in and out of her, cooling her lungs. The blade was somehow back on her hip, pretending it had never left. She raised her head and saw Madigan standing in front of her again.

"That should hold you over for a while."

The door revealed itself and Alan walked in to clear up the remains of his earlier manifestation.

"Don't worry about Alan here, we'll bring him back good as new. I, however, would be a different story. Luckily, I programmed in some visual assists back in the early days. Very useful. Of course, at the time I just thought they looked cool."

From behind his back Madigan produced a small rectangular mirror. "You haven't seen yourself in quite some time, have you?"

He angled the mirror and Cass saw her face slant down into view.

At least, it was almost her face. The shape was recognisable, the set of the eyes and hair, but the rest was off. The skin was pale and drawn, similar to the vampires she no longer needed to avoid. Her cheekbones pushed out, tight and shiny over her small tense mouth, pointing the way to the real change. The lips. They were bright red and shining with a strange glow.

"It's a measure of the spread, of how far gone you are. And when the hunger comes over you, they change again, deepening to almost black, dark as blood in the moonlight."

Her image flashed away as Madigan slid the mirror back behind himself. "You don't have much time."

His arms came back in front, empty now. Sleight of hand. How could she trust anything in this place?

"You can't. You can only trust your instincts, which have led you here before it was too late. They have been honed out there in the dark. You have been honed. Did you never wonder what the purpose was? The goal at the end of the road you walk?"

He motioned to the wall where a monitor now sat. On its screen a dark figure stood in the centre of the lane, shrouded in black. Cass felt an instant shock of recognition. Quarters. The figure she saw with him. The woman that turned towards her.

"You're becoming more like her with every kill. Less like a user, more like a virus. That is the purpose. You contain some of her already, and thanks to your peculiar talents, you have the power to stop her before she ends it all. Perhaps you alone."

The screen changed now to a long shot of the Grid, glowing in the distance.

"We brought these powers to bear on ourselves, perhaps we deserve what is coming. The River will still be here long after we have gone."

The monitor began to change, to grow. Cass was transfixed as Madigan's voice faded into the background.

"It's not so bad being stranded here, really. I know I can never go back. This is my universe now. Sometimes I wonder if the River has always been there. Other times I question if it has ever been there at all."

The wall itself was the picture now, then the room around her, then it was gone. She was standing in the street, staring off at the Grid in the distance. Madigan's voice was a whisper in her useless ears. "What is life without goals, after all?"

***

Poe didn't try to argue, just pushed his hands down on the arms of his chair to get up and froze.

Nothing happened. He looked down at his legs and all he could see was a writhing mass of cables covering his lap, throbbing with power, snaking in and around his limbs, slowly tightening their grip.

Gretchen was smiling down at him now, and he noticed the soft piping music surrounding them. "It's not time to leave, detective. I told you; you have to help me find him. It's time we took a proper look inside to see what you really remember."

The music was growing in volume as the cables slid further up his body, paralysing him with their touch.

"Memories are difficult things to trust, especially when caged in words. I find it best to go directly to the source, hmm? You can struggle if you like, but it won't help you in the slightest."

His arms now refused to move as the cables reached his hip. They had formed themselves into the one organ, a giant mouth slowly swallowing him whole. Gretchen's words continued to drone on in the distance as his brain drowned in panic. "The man we're looking for used to like talking about memory. He considered himself a collection of memories surrounding a body, not a whole being. Constantly confused by his actions of the past. That was the line. Madigan liked that one, we all did."

Poe's brain was paralysed with fear. It couldn't react at all, just sit and listen and watch with horror as the great mouth crept up his chest, up towards his face.

"The connection between body and brain is a complicated one. Where, for instance, do you draw the line between thought and emotion? Which is a by-product of which? Changes to the body affect both, and what is memory but a collection of thoughts and emotions stored away in a part of the body, hmm? All very interesting questions."

The music had to be doing it, had to be altering his brain, giving him visions. It had to be a hallucination, but all he could think about was the panic rushing through him.

"Music is a powerful retriever of memories. So is taste, and smell. All the senses. Fear is another one often overlooked. We remember moments of panic very clearly. Time slows down as our senses expand to soak every detail in. Likewise, fear can help us sink back into the past to find what we have lost. Adrenaline, norepinephrine, serotonin, dopamine. The neurotransmitters, the chemicals which make up thought, all the same chemicals the amygdala releases in the moment of panic, in the fight-or-flight response. All very closely linked to the major hallucinogens too. Mescalin and adrenaline are almost chemically identical."

The mouth was at his neck now. Poe couldn't even move his head to strain his face away from it.

"Madigan knew, we all knew what we were capable of. He was always too soft to use what knowledge he had. I know better, hmm? These weapons are necessary on our little quest. Don't worry, it won't take long."

Poe's eyes rolled up in his head as darkness slid over him.

***

Body of Christ. That phrase had always had a special resonance for Adlai. This is my body; this is my blood. You went up to the priest, hands clasped in front of you, trying not to look foolish, feeling all eyes on you. You said the magic word and then you ate it. You ate Christ's body. What kind of fucked up thing was that to teach an eight-year-old?

Adlai felt separated enough from his body as it was. It was a vehicle, this collection of cells and organs which made up consciousness. Nothing more. When he was young, he was constantly running into things, cutting himself, watching his blood flow out onto the schoolyard. Never anything serious, he never lost a limb, but he didn't think that would have made a difference. Adlai was his mind, not his body. The body was unimportant.

Wasn't that the whole point of religion when you got right down to it? You attempt to transcend the physical, rise into the spiritual. Deny yourself physical pleasures, or sins if you prefer, to allow your consciousness to rise above it. What Adlai built in VR made this possible without sacrifice. You could step out of your body without suffering. Stop being the animal you didn't wish to be.

Of course, by the time most users came into the River they were adults, had spent their entire lives wrapped up in themselves, didn't want to leave their bodies behind. They took them with them, or at least the idea of them, the form. Looked the same on one side of the port as the other, with perhaps a few minor adjustments here and there. Bigger shoulders, better skin, slimmer waist. All cosmetic. The same form generally remained. It was unusual for a user to change sex online for any length of time, let alone species.

But then why should we expect any different? How often do you dream you are someone else, something else? Hardly ever. Never, for most people. Their being, their mind is so caught up in their body shape, so affected by the way they look and feel that they simply cannot accurately imagine what being truly different would feel like. More to the point, they simply don't want to.

Users went so far as to bring their ports over, all the better to mimic reality. Adlai had seen them on the River, users jacking in as if they were on the other side of the divide, using their ports to jump deeper into the looking glass of VR. A virtual experience of virtual reality.

It wasn't until later, when the fields were introduced and the ports really opened for everyone, when the kids got inside, that the real freaks arrived. Children who were uncomfortable with themselves, especially teenagers, transformed themselves completely when handed the freedom to do so. The VR worlds took on a new slant. They became fascinating, messy, dangerous places. Jungles.

We all brought ourselves along for the ride, our issues and worries, our prejudices and obsessions. The River magnified them all. It was a way to exert some sort of control over life and its multitudinous confusion.

You were no better. Gave yourself a hat and a pipe and a superior attitude.

Adlai stared out the window at the rain sheeting down.

Long ago now.

Much in the way the physical and mental sides never fit together, so the past never seemed to belong either. It was a source of confusion. He couldn't make sense of it, couldn't identify with the person he used to be, remember what he thought or did. Why he acted. There was no whole self-link between then and now. Life was a whirl of confusion.

Cigarettes, though, cigarettes ground you. Much like alcohol.

He pulled a single cigarette from behind his ear and put it in his mouth. A moment later the bartender reached across and lit it for him.

They drag you back into your body. Remind you where you are. That's why so many drunks smoke. Stops them wandering off from themselves, getting lost in the jumble of their ideas.

God was a smoker; Adlai had understood that a long time ago.

"The question is," the bartender had moved away again, but Adlai continued despite him. "What type of cigarettes does he prefer?"

***

Cass was standing in the street, Madigan's warehouse at her back, the glow of the Grid the only highlight on the horizon that stretched out in front of her. Raindrops streaked down her face and body, tingling as they leapt off her fingertips.

He'd shown her the target. Her target. The figure who appeared at the crash site, the one who took Quarters away from her, who turned her into this. What was "this" anyway? What was she? A machine, a hunter. A tool. A blade. She looked down at the curved knife dangling from her hip, glistening in the rain. It had changed her, twisted her, used her. The hunger was all she had left.

But it wasn't just hunger, it was power. Power to alter the world around her, power to take down those that threatened her. She was capable of feats she'd never even imagined, things that shouldn't be possible out here. Did it matter where the power came from? Cass smiled as she felt the now familiar surge of adrenaline pump into her shoulders and spine.

It was hers now.

Cass turned and sprinted for the closest wall. Solid brick, it stretched three storeys high without a break. She wasn't sure what she would do but knew that was no longer important. She was a creature of instinct.

Even its creator, even Madigan had feared her. She had seen it in his eyes. She was more than just a tool. She was her own weapon. She was the River Blade. This was her playground.

As her feet left the ground and hit the wall she kept moving, pumping her legs, running vertically up the wall, splashing the water that ran down the outside of the building back up into her grim face. Just keep up the speed until the ledge appears.

The overflowing gutter swam into reach and she grabbed it with both hands, pushing her legs with a final surge out from the wall, allowing her momentum to flip herself over and around. As she passed vertical she let go, pulling into a crouch and bringing her feet back in underneath her. Her soles slapped down on the slate tiles of the roof and she crouched there perfectly still, scanning the surrounding land.

Now she just had to find her prey. Find the one who took everything away.

Nothing. Anyone who'd just seen her run up a three-storey building would know better than to make themselves visible, but it was more than that. There was no one here, she could feel it.

Even that sense, the one she'd always had, the ability to sense life and meaning, it too was heightened now. She could feel the scan as physical reach out around her, searching out all the dark corners for life. Nothing escaped it.

Cass slowly stood up and began to walk. There was only one place to go.

The bar where she'd run into the clone, where she'd felt that strange presence of power. It was east from here, directly towards the Grid. And after that? She could keep going, up to the walls of the Grid itself. Use her new powers to tear them down, let the users inside taste what it meant to be free.

Madigan had told her that was her goal. That was what the blade was for. What she was for. She'd seen it behind his eyes, if not in his words. The River Blade was made to take down the Grid.

She was a weapon, a virus that needed to feed. And when another predator wanders into your grounds, you have to take it out.

It and anything else that gets in your way.

***

Poe opened his eyes. At least, he thought he did. There was no sign the signal had been received in his brain; everything was liquid darkness. He tried to move and again couldn't tell if he was successful or not. His hands touched nothing as they moved, not even each other.

He was floating in black ink, everything around him muted and intangible. Was this death?

She'd drugged him, of course, or piped in music to do the equivalent, altering his brain to her wishes. The cables, the mouth, none of that had been real, it couldn't have been. Hallucinations, brought on by panic and loss of control. He wasn't in some being's stomach; he was inside himself. "Adlai?"

There was no reply, just more searching darkness. For the first time in his memory, he felt truly alone.

He blinked and found himself sitting in the captain's waiting room. The secretary was there, typing away. "The captain will see you in just a moment."

Same voice, same outstanding legs. Was this memory?

"The captain will see you now."

Poe stood automatically and walked into the office.

There was the green lamp, the menacing shadows, the hunched figure you couldn't quite make out.

"Anything to report?"

As if by instinct his mind relaxed and it was all sucked out of him, poured out and sifted through.

Pickpockets, shadows, hunters, dreamers, clones, Madigan, visions, songs, conversations. He felt a sense of dissatisfaction and a tightening on his brain as though a fist clenched around it. The fingers dug deeper, churning up what was hidden and forcing it to the surface. He caught fleeting glimpses before they sank back down. A crash site, a figure watching him from a rooftop, a bar. Poe no longer recognised the flashes, yet they were somehow familiar. A figure in a seat, staring out the window, drink in hand.

"Thank you, Poe, that will be all."

The voice was different now, more feminine. He was dismissed. He turned to walk out and darkness engulfed him.

He spun around but there was nothing of the office, nothing of the captain. There was only blackness, and emptiness, as if what had held him in its hand had suddenly dropped him and left him alone to die.

And something else. Something growing. He could feel and hear it at the same time. A short tune he'd heard before. Where was that coming from?

Poe couldn't identify the notes, but he could almost see them. They were growing, leaping on top of each other in turn, becoming larger and larger to take over his entire field of vision. Opening something up he didn't want to let in.

He needed to wake up. Had to wake up. He didn't want to be there when she came.

As soon as the thought formed in his head it leapt out of his mind and burned a hole in the darkness. A door. She was coming. Poe tried to close his eyes and force the song out of his head, but it danced out of his reach. It was no use.

He opened his eyes and stared straight into her face.

***

Adlai still remembered her face. It was burned into his memory, her eyes, the slanted, mischievous grin. He sometimes wondered if it had all just been down to bad timing. He was lonely, wasn't thinking straight. If he'd met her at any other time he would have walked away immediately.

But he hadn't. He'd strung along, planning, conspiring, wrapping himself tighter and tighter in her net, until when it came time to break free, to finally sever the bonds holding them all back, he'd hesitated. Out of fear.

"Fear is the child's bedfellow."

Who had said that anyway? He couldn't remember. Just another quote drifting around in his head, popping up from the soup now and then.

What had he been afraid of? Losing it all? Death?

Awareness of death is what differentiated man from the animals, right back to biblical times. Adam and Eve eating from the tree of knowledge. What did it teach them other than the fact of their own mortality?

And then Freud, that other great religious figure, what did he say? That man defeats his own death instinct by killing others. No wonder so much out there on the River had become what it had. Glorified arenas, dark, twisting streets, all the better to hunt in. Fuck it, good luck to them.

The bourbon still burned, it never stopped burning. He could adjust it, but would that ruin the whole effect? You had to be careful in this place, perched between the two worlds. Once done things weren't so easily fixed.

"Luck is when the guy next to you gets hit by the arrow." He knew that one. That was Aristotle. Man's basic narcissism, complete absorption with self. Games with death are okay because it will never happen to me, not in any conscious part of my brain. The unconscious can feed off the fear and breed excitement.

So, we had this. A dark, wet playground. Not even that. A classroom perhaps. They had even introduced a teacher.

It wasn't worth feeling guilty about. No, only the Separation was worth that. The ripping away of users from their avatars, their dreams, the amputation of fantasy, leaving both sides floating free like a kite snapped and careening in the wind. Knowing it was necessary didn't make it any easier to deal with.

He'd done it to himself too, of course. He could have exempted himself, it would have been easy, but he knew he had to follow through. Had to live with the consequences of his actions. No good holding others up to high ideals and then failing to do so yourself.

Let his other side go, the construct he'd formed for himself. The eccentric detective.

And now he found himself here on the edge, surrounded on both sides by empty shells. You could see it in every eye you bothered to look into.

Is death really the main, overriding fear in life? Perhaps it's loneliness.

Every now and then he could drop in for a visit, couldn't he? See how things were. He wouldn't intervene, just watch. Maybe his presence itself would be enough.

Just for a moment, a second, just to feel it again, just to see through those eyes.

Adlai stared up at the window and felt his eyes glaze over as the code ran through his head.

He wasn't far away, which was surprising. Off-Grid, away from the bright lights. Somewhere familiar, from the past. Very familiar. Somewhere dangerous.

Adlai opened his eyes.

***

Poe's eyes opened.

A wave of nausea rolled up and down his body, and he coughed and tried to sit up. His head hit a wooden beam and he lay back down quickly and concentrated on not throwing up. He was back, dragged back from oblivion. He blinked his eyes to make sure they were still working.

Eyes, that's what he'd last seen. Her eyes. She'd taken him, pulled him down into the blackness but he'd been brought back.

"Feeling better, sir?"

Warmth flooded him as he realised he was no longer alone. "Adlai? Where have you been? You had me worried for a while there."

"I'm not quite sure myself, sir – I could see, but I was trapped, locked in somehow."

"Yes. Well, I know how you feel."

Poe lifted his legs and met the same wooden board. He was boxed in. What had she done to him?

The visit to the captain, it had all been part of an elaborate fantasy constructed around him, a music fuelled vision to drop his guard and let her in to the deepest parts of his mind. Then she'd found what she wanted and left him for dead. Buried him here, to be forgotten.

But he'd woken up. One minute there had been nothing, the next he was back. It was as though something had sparked into his brain, powering it up again, getting the cylinders flying.

Something familiar.

He had another flash of memory, something Gretchen had dragged up. A lone figure at a bar, someone she was looking for. There was more though. She'd said it was his connection to the other side, his dreamer.

"Dreamer, sir?"

"I'm not too sure about that one myself, Adlai. It's something important though. Something we have to find."

She'd found what she wanted and left him to the virus. Left him to be obliterated by that song, by that woman. He'd looked into her eyes yet somehow, he was still here.

Trapped, but not for long.

Poe reared his legs back and kicked out. Light streamed in as the thin timber shattered and broke away. He sat up and looked around at the microphones and speakers lining the walls. Gretchen was gone.

The bunker was just that now, a collection of lifeless cables and stands, the spark had left it.

"The ghost in the machine."

"Sir?"

"Just something someone once told me. Come, help me make sure this place never hurts anyone again."

Poe ducked under the control table and started yanking out cables.

He was angry. Angry at himself for falling into her trap, but also angry that he didn't know what he needed to. Investigation is the uncovering of the past, revealing facts obscured by time and circumstance. It was in his nature. His purpose was to look backwards, recall what had become lost. So why couldn't he remember anything about himself?

A thick black power cable came free on the fourth attempt and he pulled it out and across the room.

Madigan had hinted something, about his pipe, said he had moved on from that character, more of a Dupin than a Holmes. Were they talking about the same thing?

He looked across the room and memorised the path to the exit. Not too far, twenty paces at most. Easy.

The visions Gretchen had shown him, what she'd claimed was the past, it had been familiar too. He'd seen it before. Why couldn't he remember?

Poe grabbed a microphone stand and curled the power cable around it. A large speaker lined the wall just within reach. It would do nicely.

He had to find that figure in the bar. His "connection". There was one place that could give him the answer. Besides, his report was overdue.

He reached back and drove the stand deep into the heart of the speaker, which let out a metallic yelp before popping and sparking as all life in the compound shorted out.

***

Cass was on another train, standing over some old man who kept trying to rub his knees up against her. She ignored him. She was lost in thoughts of the past, of what might have been.

You forget how real life is, how cold and lonely and cruel when your eyes are open. You wake up one morning and realise that after last night you're alone. What you thought could last forever has ended already.

You can tell yourself about opportunity, about fish in the sea, about making the right decision and not settling for less. It doesn't seem to help though.

What you're missing most is part of yourself, the piece you gave to them, invested in them and hoped to see grow. The view of you through their eyes, that aspect of yourself you were slowly beginning to appreciate, to love. Some people called that happiness.

That's what hurts the most.

You're left numb, disinterested. Back to the same old grind. An empty shell, slowly refilling over time, only to pour it all out again. Like a toilet cistern.

Cass smiled to herself. Listen to you. You'd think the world had ended.

She'd thought this one could last, at least for a year or two. Stop the longing for other worlds, bring her back into reality and the possibilities of life on this side. Stop her lying down every night desperately trying to find her dreams. That was all she needed, just a little time. Of course, when that year was up the story would change again.

Still, it wasn't too much to ask, was it? Since the Separation she'd been drifting along lost and had finally stumbled into someone who looked like they might be able to understand. Looked like they'd had their heart broken, their dreams taken away. Looked like they needed her too.

It had only lasted a couple of months.

She wasn't even sure why it had ended. She wasn't one of those girls constantly digging away, undermining him until he had no choice but to come crashing down into her arms. Asking him what he was thinking. Maybe that would have worked.

Cass simply got the email at work. Sitting, staring out the window at the grey sky again, waiting for a reply to keep her entertained and Bang! All over in a rush of words, like he couldn't wait to get them out, like he'd found the turn of phrase he needed, clutched at it and pulled it down over the cliff with him.

Fuck him.

You still say things like that to yourself, as though you're still tough, as though that side of you hadn't died long before this. Died when you woke up with that sound in your ears, the pillow wet from the River, or was it simply your tears?

There was a tap on her shoulder and she turned around to see an old woman talking to her. Speaking at her. She smiled apologetically and motioned to her ears. I'm deaf you see. That's why I'm standing here alone. That's why this life seems to keep failing. That's why I can't seem to be happy anymore.

The woman muttered to the man sitting down about the youth of today and Cass stepped aside to let her pass.

People would believe anything.

There was no guilt, no twinge of conscience. It was useful to pretend, to yourself and others. Most of the noise of this world was better left unheard.

***

The most important lesson Poe had been taught as a detective was that of Occam's razor. Do not over-complicate things. When faced with numerous possibilities, the simplest is usually correct. Poe preferred to reject this unconditionally. Leave such thinking to the other detectives, the by-the-book boys. After all, where was the fun in it?

If he was a believer in simplicity, he certainly never would have found himself here. A musician crashes off-Grid. The simplest solution? Hookers or drugs. But scratch the surface a little more and what do you find? Clones, memory cards, musical viruses, just to name a few.

Poe pulled out his notepad and skimmed over things again. It was best to be prepared. Besides, it hadn't all fallen into place yet. The more things soaked in, the quicker they would make sense.

He was sitting in the captain's waiting room, doing what it was designed for. The secretary was there again, same girl, same dress, same legs. Poe ignored her. No point being rude.

She didn't seem to feel the same way, however, and hadn't taken her eyes off him since he'd appeared. Well, isn't that always the way? Show some interest and you get nowhere but start ignoring a girl and you become fascinating. The same rules applied in here as out there, with real girls and answering machines.

He waited for Adlai's reply but got nothing. Adlai wasn't here. He always seemed to disappear when it was time to meet the boss. Perhaps it was for the best.

Poe was alone with his thoughts and the small puddle forming at his feet.

That stopped him.

Why was a small puddle forming at his feet? It wasn't wet here, this was just a projection of the captain's office, a construct to allow easy data transfer. He could be up to his neck in water off-Grid, none of it should appear here. He tapped his foot in the puddle and splashed water up onto his pants.

"The captain will see you now."

Poe ignored her. Where had this water come from? Why had they bothered recreating this virtually?

"Detective Poe?"

His clothes, his belongings, they stayed with him to ease the experience, to make the process of reporting in seem more natural. There was no need for this.

"Detective Poe, please!"

He looked up and stared at the secretary. She was almost on her feet, pushed up from her desk on thin, quivering arms. As he looked, she relaxed back down into the chair.

"The captain will see you now."

Poe stood and walked over to the door, not taking his eyes off her. She'd reacted to him. Looked almost human.

He noticed a single strand of hair had escaped the clasp holding it back and was drifting down over her eyes. As he stepped past, he reached down and brushed it back off her face. Then he stopped. There was sweat beaded on her forehead.

"Poe!"

This time it was the captain himself; you couldn't keep him waiting. Poe swung away and continued into the office. "Sir?"

"Poe, take a seat."

This wasn't making any sense. Why would a virtual answering machine react like that? What was the point? So like a human.

The captain's words registered and Poe stared at him.

"Excuse me, sir?"

"You heard me, sit down. It's high time we explained some things, and I always find bad news much easier to take sitting down."

***

Adlai remembered Gretchen's voice the most. The sound of it. How much she enjoyed using it, threatening and cajoling and most of all, making speeches.

"The time has come. Time to rise up against the corporate gatekeepers who hide behind their walls and segregate those who threaten their true power to the darkness outside the Grid. Time to seize control of the hardware, let it be shared among the many, rather than the few. Time to fight back."

Gretchen was standing before them, her voice ringing out as she paced on her own stage. Adlai didn't mind. It made what he had to do easier when she was like this.

The others turned around and waited for his decision. Hound and Strafe standing together as always, fingering the thin blades Madigan had forged for them. Madigan himself standing further back, grin fixed in place, hands rubbing each other for comfort. They were a sorry lot.

"Very well. We begin tonight. You all know the plan."

He turned and walked out and hoped it looked dramatic.

The plan was a simple one. Meet at a point right on the border of the Grid, send Hound and Strafe in to open things up and divert most of the heavy attention. Then he, Madigan and Gretchen would burrow in and head straight for the heart of it. Hack the system and bring it all down. That was the plan. At least, that was what he'd told them.

Adlai wanted one last walk before it was all taken away. He knew no matter what happened tonight things would be very different from now on.

The streets were empty, and he was left undisturbed as he wandered through the darkness and the rain. What would become of them all after tonight? Would they even remember?

He walked and let his thoughts follow his feet along the road. His eyes were heavy, as they always seemed to be now. He missed sleep. Hours spent floating in multiplying realities until you can no longer distinguish between work and dreams, or if there had ever been a difference between the two. Technology had merged and confused them.

He was tired. Tired of watching it all go wrong, tired of planning and scheming and all of it. He just wanted to sit and think for a while now. Have a drink. Let the world pass him by while he sat and watched.

These snippets of memory, the flashes of dialogue, the glimpses into his past self, they were why he was here, sitting at the bar. He no longer doubted they had been real, perhaps warped by time and memory, but real, nonetheless. He was here now. They were… somewhere else.

"Another one for you, Jack. 'The world of human aspiration is largely fictitious, and if we do not understand that, we understand nothing about man.'"

So perhaps his memories weren't one hundred per cent accurate. What of it?

"Know who said that? No, me neither."

There was too much emotion tied up in his thoughts, he could no longer untangle the two. It was better just to forget. Forget yourself. Forget the past. Forget everything. Leave the memories to those who can enjoy them. Look out the window and watch your dreams pass by.

***

Cass froze as she stared across the bar.

That's him, isn't it? No need to even ask the question – that's him. Light a cigarette and think about it but the answer won't change. He's been here a while. Maybe you didn't recognise him at first, so maybe he decided to do the same. Is doing the same. Will do the same from now on. Besides, he's with friends. You don't know them and never will.

This was where you first met him. Kane. Drunk in a bar, surrounded by those too set in their ways or simply too downright poor to visit the River. Here to drink their dreams out and away. It served the same purpose. As for you, you couldn't go back there, not since the Separation. There was no catching your dreams.

It certainly wasn't cheap. There were still those who only ever experienced glimpses, perhaps a few minutes on a hired port, subsidised, wandering around the Grid, heads in the air, dazzled by the few freaks who still bothered to congregate at general stations. Cheap show-offs, too scared to wander outside the safety net of the Grid where they would be such easy pickings. They were a joke.

No, better to hang out somewhere like this. Surround yourself with others, all fooling yourselves that you're not missing out on anything.

He was just another one, at the time. You talked about bullshit, fed each other the lines about work, life, dreams. He was a musician. Neither of you took it too seriously. Then later, the next morning, you were glad to be rid of him. He was more evidence of your fall, stains that needed washing off. You forgot him.

Then again, not much later. It was convenient. Just as good, just as forgettable. Then again.

He became sort of a habit. Almost something more, but it had ended in the fumbled, confused way these things always seemed to end. She still wasn't sure why.

So, what's the problem now? Now, when you see him here again, looking good, looking really good – maybe that's just the drink, 'cause really, he's always been just what he's been. A distraction. An interlude. Is it just that you haven't figured out what the next act is yet?

The sex was good though. Primal, like you both needed to step sideways out of the drag of life. You both said what you wanted and got it, which is how it should be. But then once it happens that way, you're both left wondering. If him, why not that next guy as well? Why not the one after? It's only later – too late – that you realise how rare those moments are.

Maybe he hasn't seen you yet. You look different, more together. More confident, more refined. Fuck, you just look older.

Cass took a long drink and stared at the mark the glass left on the treated wood of the bar.

It's not fair to feel rejection when you're still alone. This feeling should be left to others, the ones for whom it's supposed to mean something, the ones who have something to lose. This programme is no longer meant to be running in my system.

Moments like these are character forming, that's what they used to say. The saying was out of date, characters were now formed in other ways, other worlds and possibilities.

On the way home it started raining, and for a moment it was perfect, just like the River. But then a stray cat wandered up close to her leg, something that would never happen so innocently out there.

She bent down to stroke it, but it scampered away.

***

Poe sat and kept very still. He had that feeling again, when you know something big is about to hit you and all you can do is wait and try to ride it out.

"We've been monitoring your progress, Edgar, and I must admit I've been rather impressed."

Edgar? That was a first. And compliments. This was going to be bad, just get it over with.

"The answers will come, just be patient. Allow me to explain."

Poe sat in his seat and quietly dripped.

"You know in the past we've made an effort to keep things very… regimented here, when you visit us. Give off the impression of a controlled environment. Professional. Virtual. Take Wendy, for example."

The captain gestured to the door. "Always the same dress, always the same lines. Just like a machine. Of course, we rely somewhat on prior expectations. You provide them, we try to live up to them."

The water pooling at his feet seemed to drop sharply in temperature. Here it comes.

"The end result is that you believe this to be a virtual environment. The flip side being that outside of here is reality. The interesting question is that for someone of your... upbringing, shall we say? For someone like you, what constitutes reality anyway?"

Poe tapped his foot in the puddle and finally looked up. "This is real, all of this." It wasn't a question.

"Correct. These little side trips of yours, ports out of the city into my office. They've been seen as small slices of the virtual in a complicated reality, when the truth is exactly the reverse."

It was true, he felt that uncomfortable surge up his spine that always appeared when the veil had been ripped back.

"Edgar Poe. You have another name, of course. A middle name. Allan."

Allan. Alan. Just like Madigan's clones.

"You can accept this because you already knew it to be true. You've glimpsed the history of your virtual universe; you've seen what some users are capable of within its limits. Were capable of, I should say. We'd like to think we snuffed out such threats a long time ago. Obviously, troublemakers still appear once in a while, which is where you come in handy."

"To hunt them for you."

"Precisely, Edgar. You have a knack for finding the truth, no matter how hidden or twisted it may be. It's increasingly difficult to find men like you these days. We simply don't design them like you anymore."

Design. He was code, a programme used to chase down rogue users in a virtual universe for his masters out here in reality. He was nothing more than software.

"Come, come, Poe, don't be so hard on yourself. Many would disagree with your basic assumptions, perhaps most of all the man who designed you in the first place. The River is a far more interesting place these days than anywhere off it. Everyone spends at least a few hours each day under its spell. Only the old guard like myself still cling to the clear separation between it and the world outside anymore. To be honest I can see their point, I just have a hard time changing definitions at this age. Call me stubborn."

The man who designed me? Poe caught a glimpse again, a flash of a hunched figure in a bar. "Why?"

"Why are we telling you all this now? As I said, you knew all of this already, really, you just couldn't bring yourself to face the facts. We're all stubborn in our own little ways. This is the push off the cliff needed before the final meeting. You're getting close to our goal. Understanding could make the difference between success and failure."

Poe dropped his head and stared at his feet. What was he seeing, really? Could any sense be trusted anymore? A flash of intuition ran through him. "The Grid. This is about the Grid. You're worried about it."

The captain leant forward and rested his hands very precisely on the desk in front of him. "You see this, this is what concerns me. I find these moments very disturbing. Independent thought. Connections made, links felt. Such talents are the domain of conscious beings, Poe. Of course, such moments are precisely why you are so useful to us. You survive because of this usefulness, Poe, never forget that."

For a cold moment the captain stared at Poe, stared into him, at all the future possibilities. "Yes, this is about the Grid. We all have bosses, Poe, those who have power over us. These bosses of mine become concerned when something they can't control threatens their existence. That's where you come in."

***

Cass crouched on the rooftop and stared coldly at the door to the bar. She'd been there for minutes, hours, days. She was waiting for something. Figures had wandered in and out of the bar, but it wasn't yet time. She could wait as long as it took.

Finally, someone came out and she felt her body wake up. A single male, youngish, hunched shoulders against the rain. Stumbling a little, maybe exaggerating it. Doesn't look around, just heads straight east, towards the Grid, oblivious to all around him.

Cass waited and watched. This bait would be taken, she could feel it.

The air vibrated around her as if someone had grabbed the world and pulled it taut, flicked it with their fingernail to make it hum.

The figure in the street slowed and then stopped, staring off to his left at the dark alley. He began to back away. This was it.

Cass leapt across to the next building, then up to the nearest power line and slid across the street on it. She hit the roof running and leaned over to look down into the alley. There was nothing.

The man had backed right up against the far side of the street, a featureless brick building holding him up. His face was twisted into a mask of terror and panic. He crept slowly across the wall until his fingers found the edge of a windowsill, then turned and pulled himself up quickly. There were no stumbles now. He was pushed back against the wall, hands splayed outwards, trying to disappear into the brick itself, eyes staring madly down at the ground.

Cass scanned again but there was nothing. Just that familiar vibration in the air. Same as earlier, same as with Quarters. She was here, she was close, but Cass couldn't sense her.

There was a way inside it, there had to be. As soon as Cass had the thought, she knew what the answer was. The blade leapt up into her hand.

She didn't bother with the power lines this time, just jumped the two storeys down, flew out from the rooftop to land lightly on her feet in front of the terrified man. Then two more steps and she was beside him, blade against his throat. The man's eyes didn't move from where they were fixed. She let the blade dig in.

The world around her warped, shifted two feet to the left. She looked down at her hands and they were someone else's, a man's – the man's – and beyond them, underneath them, the ground was moving.

She looked closer and shrank back as it became clear. The street was covered in rats, swarms of them, crawling on top of one another, burying each other in their eagerness to reach him. To reach you. They were hungry.

Their black fur was wet from the rain and sticky with blood, teeth and claws dripping with it, fighting each other, piling on top of each other and getting ever higher on the wall. Just another foot now.

The first one made it to the narrow ledge and he kicked out at it. They were enormous, at least a foot and a half long, heavy bodied. Moments later another came, then another. He couldn't knock them all back down and felt the first diseased fangs sink into his ankle.

The pain pushed him further back against the wall, then the second and third bites dropped him, face first, into the slathering pile. He felt hungry mouths chew into his cheeks.

The blade clattered down onto the road and suddenly the world around her was clear. Cass was on her knees, sucking in air, hands covering her face. She looked up at the street, but it was empty. Everything had gone. The man had gone.

Taken. Taken by her, by the vision that she was there to face, that she'd been able to do nothing about.

Cass felt out to the blade and wrapped her fingers around its hilt. There was no blood on the blade, and it hummed with hunger. It wanted to feed. Well, there was only one thing for it now. They would feed again soon.

She strode up to the bar door and pushed it open.

***

Poe stood frozen in front of the captain, the words drilling into his mind, breaking things free.

"We're not unaccustomed to dealing with threats from the outside. From the day the first tower of the Grid rose up there have been those who would bring it down. Some see the organization of power as inherently evil, despite the good it does. Fortunately, there have always been those who would fight on our side, if only for personal gain.

"Virus attacks have occurred in the past too. Yes, Poe, that's what this is, make no mistake. The victims you've stumbled across are casualties in a war waged against the Grid. It's only a matter of time before the focus turns and sharpens. The reason none of these attacks have been successful is that we have always been willing to fight back, to raise the stakes. We stay one step ahead.

"Of course, lately things have become more difficult. The talents we employed have left; the machines have slowed. We are vulnerable, Poe. We need your help."

Poe stared at the man in front of him, leaning forwards, suddenly speaking of the Grid as a though it was part of him. For a moment he wondered when that line had been crossed, when the man outside had become another cog in the great machine. He was no longer an individual. Perhaps he would be better off on the other side of the world, the side of dreams and possibility. At least he could still dream himself. "I have my own reasons for doing this. Let's just say our goals share a common path."

"Of course, of course. You've seen glimpses already; you need to know more. That drive is your strength, Poe, we rely on such characteristics. Such predictability. It is rare these days."

He hadn't said a thing, but they knew it all. Knew of the visions he'd seen, knew of the bar and the man slumped against it who somehow sat at the centre of this all. Of course, they knew it all. He wondered if they were capable of understanding.

"Think of yourself as bait, Poe, nothing more. We need to draw this virus out to cleanse it completely. Then we can cauterise and move on. Perform your duty and leave the answers to us."

Poe found himself on his feet and realised he'd been dismissed. He turned and walked out of the office, knowing he'd never see it again.

"The search for understanding doesn't always lead where you might expect, Poe. Never forget what you are."

Was that a friendly piece of advice or a warning? He decided he no longer cared.

The office door swung slowly shut behind him and he was left staring at the stark waiting room.

The secretary sat primly, clattering away on the ancient typewriter. He felt he should say something, make a final statement to sum up the years he'd spent here. Had it been years, or only moments? It didn't matter, nothing here did. Briefly he wondered if they'd even remember him.

He leant down, grabbed her chin and kissed her roughly on the lips.

A moment later he was on his way out. His lips were warm, and the office behind him had fallen silent.

***

Adlai had been tortured by nightmares for as long as he could remember.

When they had first started happening regularly, when the nightmares first began to take hold, his parents had been worried. They couldn't help but notice it. He'd wake up silently screaming, soaked in sweat, then pad into their room and crawl into the warmth between them. The safety. Who could protect you from the horrors of the night better than the two who brought you into this world?

Because his parents were who they were it wasn't long before doctors were involved, then psychiatrists. He remembered some of the tests. They were fun. You could see where they were trying to go, and you tried to give the right answers. Make the decisions easier for everyone.

He knew even then they couldn't help. One of the doctors had left the door slightly open when addressing his mother. Adlai had memorised the words. He had, "a psychological predisposition to thin boundaries, arising from feelings of lack of control, common in children of his age. A tendency towards schizophrenia." His mother had leaned back on the desk, her hand to her mouth.

The nightmares didn't go away, he just stopped fighting them. Started looking into them, investigating them. They were powerful things, expanding your imagination and sensitivity, opening up other worlds and ideas. In only a few more years he could open up those worlds for real.

No schizophrenia had ever developed, at least, none that he was aware of. His marks were good, he had no social problems, no social life at all really, so his parents saw nothing obvious to worry about and pushed it back into the attic of their minds. He was less sure, but let it ride. Considering his later work, it was probably something he should have thought more about. It could be said, looking back, that instead of confronting his own problems he'd forced every other user into a world of multiple personalities. Broke down the boundaries between fantasy and reality, waking and dreaming, sexuality and aggression. It was what people wanted.

Besides, by that time the world had completely lost its marbles.

"Do it."

Hound cut the blade directly into the wall of the building, pulled it around in a rough circle and kicked the hole clear. They crowded their heads in and stared into the darkness.

"Okay, onwards."

Gretchen was driving them on as always. Adlai paced behind them, keeping up but always a few steps back. Let them think of it as cowardice. Pretty soon it wouldn't matter what they thought.

They climbed through and headed for the next wall, where Strafe this time began cutting, Hound standing watch on his shoulder. There was a way to go yet before they were inside the walls, but this was the only option they had. Approaching the Grid from any of the alleys would be fruitless. The lights would just get further away as they approached. No, the only way back in was through the walls.

There had been no alarm triggered, at least no sign of one yet. Madigan still flinched with each cut, and examined the blades carefully after each successful breach, looking for some sign of damage or corruption. He seemed more surprised than anyone that they were holding up so well. They were spotless.

Gretchen was impatient, pushing them to hurry. It was more than mere nerves for her though, it was an addict's hunger, driving her on towards what she saw as the ultimate power.

Three walls later and they were right on the edge of it. Adlai could feel them closing in, but the others showed no sign of awareness. One more wall was all it would take.

Hound cut through and dived forwards, almost in one move. The beam meant for his chest burnt harmlessly past them and melted the far wall. Adlai looked up from where he found himself on the floor and saw Strafe and Hound force their way through into the darkness, firing as they went. They disappeared then, driving the security forces back and leading them away. It was the last Adlai saw of them.

He never did find out what had happened to them. They must have been caught. Had to have been. Whatever became of them, the ploy had worked. Madigan, Gretchen and he had been left unmolested, able to walk straight in under the walls, straight to the heart of the Grid, where everything was possible.

This drink in front of him, he could take it up again, drink it, put it down and wait for it to be refilled. Or light a cigarette and throw it against the wall. Or push himself up and leave the bar, go out into the rain and darkness and find something real to occupy his time. Something more than mere memories and regrets. These were all possibilities. Some were just more likely than others.

***

The door swung slowly open and Cass was left staring at an empty hotel room. Single bed, grey TV facing it. All the usual misery and loneliness seeping in through the walls.

There was a hint of muzak in the air, as if an elevator was left stuck on her floor. The tune was familiar, tickling the back of her ears, almost a lullaby.

There was someone on the bed now. Her niece, Sally. Sitting there happily, swinging her legs. Looking up at her.

She knew she was dreaming. Sally was dead, drowned in the accident. Her screams had haunted Cass's sleep for years. Why was she here?

Cass tried to step into the room, but something held her back, stopped her legs from following orders. Sally could see the problem. She hopped down from the bed and walked over, clasped Cass's hand in hers and smiled as she dragged her inside.

Now she was in bed. The music was louder, or was it just the darkness of the room that gave this illusion, this power to the sound?

Cass opened her eyes. She was naked, curled on her side. She'd woken from a dream, a dream where her niece had come back from the dead to show her something, to reassure her perhaps. There hadn't been any malice.

There was someone's hand in hers, someone's arm over her shoulder. It felt warm and right. It felt like the last few minutes of sleep before a working day. The dread was already building.

If she stayed here, not thinking, just lying in the warmth, she could be happy.

The music had gained in volume again. It was loud enough to wake you, though the figure next to her didn't stir. Maybe it was just in her head, just her own soundtrack. She couldn't remember if she was supposed to be able to hear or not.

She had to look; had to see who it was. It felt like him, though that was impossible.

Cass lifted her head but couldn't turn. The music was rising again, becoming painful now, throbbing in her ears. It had to be leaking out of her head, pouring back out of her ears and down on to the pillow. It had to wake whoever it was.

Her neck was frozen in place. The dream didn't want her to see, didn't want it to end. She knew as soon as she looked it would be over, but still she had to. She closed her eyes and concentrated.

There was an audible crack as she finally snapped her head around. The music vanished and she was left alone in bed, properly awake now, staring down at an empty pillow.

Maybe he was scared too. Maybe it had been his dream she'd lain with, been with. Maybe they could still hold something like that together in the dark, his dream and hers. Maybe that could be enough.

Cass lay her head back down on the pillow and closed her eyes, waiting to be taken away.

***

Poe walked along the middle of the street with a spring in his step.

This was a one-way trip, the captain had as good as admitted it. He was sending him out to lure out the virus, and once that was done... well, after that the plans all became a little hazy. Nevertheless.

"It's not so bad is it, Adlai? We have to embrace our curiosity, our inquisitiveness, forget about the fears and doubts that hold us back. Some will try to tell you they are there as warning signs, there to keep you from danger. It's literally the oldest story in the book. It takes the serpent in the Garden of Eden to encourage Eve's curiosity, to convince her to eat from the tree of knowledge."

"That didn't end particularly well for Eve though did it, sir?"

"Exactly my point Adlai, exactly my point. The writers use the story of Eve to warn you against following your curiosity, against breaking rules. Do not ask difficult questions, they say, for they will only lead to trouble. And troubling answers. Those in power have always acted this way. Which begs the question..."

"Why are we being encouraged now?"

"Right! Why now? And the answer?"

Poe stared down at the ripples in the road his feet made as they trudged through the rain. Everything around him seemed sharper, more detailed, more real.

"Because we are expendable?"

"Perhaps, perhaps. I get the feeling most people are expendable in their eyes, no matter what side of this divide they talk about they're on. This reality divide."

"Because we are useful then?"

"Part of it. Not the answer as such, but a facet of it. We have our talents."

"What then?"

"Perhaps they are not so afraid of what we might find. They seem to already know all about it, or at least think they do. What was it the captain told us?"

"Uh, something about understanding not always leading somewhere."

"The search for understanding does not always lead where you might expect. Particularly poetic for a man of his leanings, if we can describe him that way, and I think that we can."

Poe had his pipe out now and began puffing on it contentedly, a slight smile on his face. There was something very comforting in things from the past. "And where does that leave us? An old piece of software and his somewhat invisible intellectual companion?"

The realisation, the words, didn't drag at him. He was happy with what he was. "It's times like these I take comfort in Madigan's words. 'One mustn't dehumanise those with the power of consciousness.'"

They walked along, lost in their own thoughts. The neon sign for the bar reached out to them through the rain. "Besides, Adlai, the more I learn about the world, the less I think such questions matter. We all find out in the end."

He tucked his pipe back into his coat and jerked his collar up around his neck. It was time. "Now let's have a drink."

***

Adlai missed sleep. Crawling into a cold bed, slowly feeling the heat radiate out from your foetal ball, then edging out into other, unexplored areas and repeating the trick. Changing the world around you, making it warm and comfortable, a suitable theatre for the dreams to come.

None of it was necessary now. The technology was there to simply lie back and let the field grab your consciousness by the hand and lead it away. Adlai preferred tradition, believed that every step taken was a necessary one. You don't skip ahead to the good stuff without sacrificing something.

People, users, were often left wondering why their dreams had become so predictable. The fact was you had to force feed most of them. Very few ever came up with something original, ever showed the wherewithal to break out on their own. And then there were those you just had to point in the right direction.

People weren't put together like they used to be. Take himself. In the past a great war or pestilence would have culled a weak man like him from existence. Instead, he had thrived. Become powerful. Become a god in VR, a leader in a universal session of psychoanalysis. He had changed people. He had done some good.

When he first started, he'd write everything down, capture it in his notebook so that no angle, no shimmer was lost. He knew he could be vague, that his memory was a sieve. A misleading analogy, really. His memory was an ocean, when new drops were added they simply dissolved away, lost in its sheer size. So he wrote things down, constructed little paper boats for them to float on the surface.

In time this led to more confusion. You weren't meant to remember all the details, there was a good reason you used to forget. Leave them there on the surface and they begin to bump into each other, to bustle and fight, force each other under. Better to let them sink on their own. If they become important later you dredge them up, like a dream. Leave the surface clear, clean and sharp. Glassy. Like this window.

He had hesitated for a moment, they all had, when faced with the darkness. Gretchen had been the first in, and they'd had to hurry to keep up once she'd stepped through. They didn't really know where they were going, but none of them could afford to get left behind.

The sounds of fighting had faded off into the distance. Strafe and Hound would buy them a few minutes at least, but still they had to be quick. There had to be a logical way in towards the centre, probably more than one, they just had to keep going until they stumbled onto it.

Madigan found the door. He cracked it open and let the light from the other side leap through. Through it was a waiting room of some sort, a large, well-furnished one with comfortable chairs and couches arranged around its walls.

Adlai broke the silence. "Well, at least they have taste."

Gretchen pushed past him then and strode into the room, looking around and daring anyone to come out to challenge her. Adlai was just about to follow when he felt a tug on his arm.

"You don't really need me anymore, do you?"

Madigan's face was still in shadow, but Adlai could imagine the expression. A small, sheepish smile, with a glint in the eye that was bit too knowing.

"No, I suppose not."

"I doubt we'll meet again."

Adlai gently pulled his arm free and walked forwards into the room. It was for the best. Perhaps Madigan could make something of himself in the twisting streets off-Grid. "One never knows out here. Take care of yourself."

"Oh, I always do."

With that he was gone, back into the shadows, back through the walls to the relative safety of the wet, dark streets that he knew.

Rainwater washed over the outside of the window and Adlai allowed himself to think of Madigan again for the first time in he didn't know how long. He must still be out there, stranded, scratching an existence out with his knowledge and his tools. He hoped he didn't regret turning back. Perhaps he was lucky and simply didn't remember.

Adlai gulped the last of his drink down and waited for the next.

Memory is the most dangerous thing of all.

***

Cass tried not to be bothered by thoughts of what he was doing now, who he was doing now, but they kept scratching at her. She'd lie in bed, hot despite the cold night air, unable to sleep, unable to dream, the field at her bedhead alive but not taking her anywhere. Not even keeping these unwelcome thoughts out.

He would be out at a gig, watching the giant screen, the lights burning back and forth across the audience. He'd see faces he liked the look of, eyes that shone with availability. They'd all find their way over to him.

He wasn't even that good looking. She could find someone much better. There was just that something in him, something that others saw, that you couldn't help but see, that attracted you and dragged you in. He took advantage of it.

None of this should bother you. Things ended for a reason. There is still a world of possibility out there for you to dive into tomorrow. Now go to sleep.

It was no good. There was a vast emptiness in her stomach, her chest, her mind. She didn't even want to find her dreams anymore, just forget reality. He'd be fucking someone else now.

Jesus, so what?

There was a light, constant rain playing across the roof and a chill in the air. It almost felt familiar. She had to go.

Cass slipped into jeans and a loose sweater, didn't bother looking at herself in the mirror, slammed the door behind her on the way out. Maybe just a walk. Wallow in self-pity for a while, enjoy it. At least you feel something.

His friends were arseholes, that was one thing. Spent their time trying to one-up each other, attacking each other behind a thin veil of humour. Drinking too much, all of them unhappy.

He was unhappy too. Lost. Perhaps that was what first attracted her to him. He looked wounded, vulnerable. The split had affected them all, even those who only visited the River intermittently. She realised later it was all part of the game. He wasn't vulnerable at all. Behind those eyes was a solid brick wall, an impenetrable fortress. She wasn't invited in.

She'd peek at him when they were kissing, or when his body tensed just before release, hoping to see something light up in there. But he was always looking away, eyes unfocused, and what she could see told her nothing. His eyes were dead.

She hoped her eyes didn't look the same way.

Back when the field would lead her away, when she spent her nights roaming the twists of the River, when she still remembered glimpses of her dreams, she hadn't needed anyone else. Her life was complete on the other side of night, she needn't worry about this one. Since the Separation, since her nights had been thrown back into reality, since her dreams had escaped her, love was the only thing she'd found worth pursuing.

That was another reason to end it. He was never going to be in the same place.

The rain felt good. She'd been walking with her head down, staring at her feet and letting her thoughts guide them along. She wasn't sure how long for.

Where was she anyway?

The dark streets around her were unfamiliar. There was something about them though – maybe she'd only ever seen this part of the city during the day. There was one building lit up on the corner.

A bar. Well, that would do. Have a drink before wandering home. If nothing else, it will settle you down.

Cass walked up to the door and tried to peer in through the windows. Covered in grime. Funny, she hadn't noticed this place before. One more of those secret little bars that seemed to pop up when no one was looking.

She shrugged and shouldered the door open.

***

Adlai turned back into the room. It was just the two of them now, he and Gretchen. He wondered briefly how long it would be before she turned on him.

If Gretchen had noticed that Madigan was no longer with them, she gave no sign. She was busy trying doors, peering down corridors, hoping to stumble onto the core.

Adlai watched for a few moments, then walked straight past her. He could feel the power emanating out from the end of the room. It was almost a heat, the air itself seemed thicker, denser. She should have been able to sense it herself, but she was too far gone by now.

He pulled open the door and immediately took a step back. It was beautiful.

The room was enormous, server after server lined up, all linked into the one display that took up the entire far wall, little lights blinking on and off as traffic moved in and out through its memory banks. Gretchen pushed past him and hurried to the machines themselves, feeling their heat and power, a rapt expression on her face. Adlai just stood there and watched the millions of dreams flicker in and out of life.

He had to do it for them. He had to act to ensure this place became more than just a playground. You can't have reality without dreams, and you can't have dreams if you live in a reality where every wish comes true. Life needs to be dark in order to be realistic. Dreams have a right to their own lives, their own tests, their own goals and fears and nightmares.

He had thought it was going to be hard, but when Gretchen yanked out a cable and the first bank of lights went out, all those dreams and lives ended, it was the easiest thing in the world. He reached into his coat, pulled out the gun he had hidden there and shot her in the spine.

Adlai dropped the gun and slumped down onto the floor. Gretchen had collapsed in a heap and lay twitching on the ground, staring straight at him. Eventually he pulled his eyes from her body, back up to the wall of lights still flickering on and off. There was still work to do.

You can't have heroes without villains, and they're not easy to find. Sometimes they have to be made. In Gretchen's words you have to break a few eggs.

Break people down. Take their dreams and squeeze them, crush them together and rip them apart in front of their eyes. Give them a reason to fight back. That's what God did with Lucifer. Created the nemesis he needed then stepped back to watch the show. Let others perform the heroics. Sat in a bar and smoked cigarettes.

"Got a light there, buddy?"

The bartender held one out immediately, but Adlai wasn't looking at him. He was watching his reflection in the window, and the figure standing directly behind him. It was about time.

Fear worked because it made us confront our own non-being. It gave us a happy thrill when the story ended and we were still there, outside its power. Our emotions triggered and then tamed by our reason.

He'd designed this entire universe to confront death. He was no longer even curious about it, let alone scared. He knew the answers already, or rather, the lack of them. The fact is, no matter what you try it flits away from you. Dances away to remain outside your field of reason.

Fear is the ultimate religious experience. To know it is to confront everything that makes life what it is. To know God. The problem is that understanding this makes it all fade back away.

When he felt the hand on his shoulder, he knew there was no point even turning around.

****

Poe pushed open the door and glanced around. It seemed harmless enough, if a little dark. There were a few figures scattered in the dark corners, but they seemed to fade into the background when you tried to pick anyone out. The only one with any presence was the hunched figure at the bar, staring out the window. Poe walked slowly towards him.

The door slammed closed behind him with a dull boom but there was no reaction, not even a raising of eyes. Usually he made something of an impression, but not in this place. This was old, you could feel it in the air, old beyond years. Everything here had been seen before.

"Perhaps I'm fading out of sight like you, Adlai."

There was no answer and Poe's feet slowed. He was alone here, like he had been in the captain's office. What did that mean? Was this place no longer part of the virtual world he lived in? Had he stepped through the divide? He felt a tingle at the base of his spine as something inside slowly awakened.

The bar. The figure at the bar still had his back to him but there was something in the set of the shoulders now, an awareness. Poe walked closer, somehow finding each step harder than the last, his feet heavier with each slow stride. The bartender stood off to one side, in a seeming daze, eyes glazed over and staring out over Poe's shoulder, out to nothing. Lost in his own world. The tingle in his spine moved north.

Just a few more steps. He was struggling to breathe now as every muscle in his body tensed. His head roared with a sudden rush of blood. He was directly behind the figure.

Over one shoulder was the window, a small dark square pin-pricked with rain. The light from the bar seemed to avoid its surface altogether, only certain images reflected back crystal clear. He saw himself standing directly behind a familiar face. It was older, more drawn, less innocent perhaps, but the same face, nonetheless. Poe lifted his hand and placed it on Adlai's shoulder.

The world disappeared and all was black.

The next thing he was aware of was music. The same music, note after note running up through his blood, forcing itself around and out of his body, taking over every cell. He felt his eyes open.

He was in a forest, morning sunlight trickling down through a cascade of leaves, ending up as a vague golden glow in the air. There was a smooth lake to his left, glinting in the sun. It was familiar.

He'd seen this place before, in a nightmare, when the music had taken control of him last time. When he'd looked around and...

Poe spun to his left and saw the young girl staring at him. She smiled once, almost naturally, and ran off giggling. He knew he had to follow her.

"You know what this is, you know this is all brought on by the virus. It doesn't make it easier, but remember it, nonetheless. Control your fear."

Poe opened his mouth but couldn't reply. It was Adlai's voice. He wasn't alone.

He was off after the girl, chasing her small white dress through the trees. His brain wouldn't allow room for anything but the chase and the music, the music that gained in volume every step.

"Almost. What you dream of as Adlai is a reflection of me as I once was, as I could have been. A dream of a dream. Some would call the ability to dream the first sign of intelligence. Perhaps this universe will be worth saving after all."

The voice and the music fought each other in his head, battling for room. He stumbled on after the girl but was losing ground. It didn't matter, she only had to lead him. Lead him to her.

"You remember. She underestimated you, underestimated both of us, that's always been her weakness. You were just a vessel, a delivery boy for her. Always far too simple minded, that girl."

Somehow he had caught up with the girl, perhaps she had waited for him. She smiled again, not so friendly this time, and disappeared around another corner. He knew what would be there.

He fought to keep the voice in his head, keep his thoughts in motion. He turned the corner and saw the woman standing there, waiting for him. Every cell froze.

The music got louder still, blasting all consciousness away as the grey skinned woman moved towards him, smiling grimly, holding him in her eyes. A final whisper of the voice drifted through him.

"Hang on."

***

Cass stood in the darkness of the bar and waited for it to happen. Nothing. No attack, no danger, no instinctive reaction. Just a dingy old room, not a single threat here.

It was just a bar. Empty, except for the bartender – a clone, even from this distance – and a lone man leaning forward on his stool, head down, staring at his glass. Neither of them had noticed her enter.

No, there was another there as well. Another man behind the one at the bar. The same figure she'd tracked here, standing with his hand on the man's shoulder.

Take them. Take them and drain them and find the answers later.

She took a step towards them and stopped. Her senses held her back. There was something in the air, an energy radiating out from them, a power. Not a threat, more of a warning.

Cass could feel her heart beating faster, the adrenaline from the kill and the possibility of more surging up her spine. The blade leapt into her hand, pulling her towards them, but she held back.

There was movement behind her as the door swung open. Cass jumped and spun in the air, flipping herself to land on a thick roof beam above the door.

Strike when they walk underneath you.

The curved blade waited just above the sill of the door but froze as the figure beneath walked through and into the dim light. Something in the shape of the body made her pause. The hair, the slope of the shoulders. It's...

A crash of glass at the bar snapped her attention away. There was something wrong. She dropped to the floor and strode towards the bar, forgetting entirely the new entry. It was obviously no threat.

The air had changed. It was warmer, heavier, more active. It wasn't music or sound this time, it was something else. The air felt alive.

She could feel the edge of the blade slice through it as she moved across the darkness. There were just the two figures, nothing had changed, but the surrounding air positively hummed with energy. Cass was almost level with them now. Instinct told her to close her eyes and suddenly she saw it.

Her. The woman who took Quarters, the one she'd seen on the street, the mother of all those nightmares. The virus. She was standing between the two figures, eyes locked on the man at the bar, glimmering in the air like an aura, like a ghost.

Cass didn't need to think. In three strides she was there, blade humming as it swept through the air. None of them reacted, not even when it brushed over the seated man, cut straight through the woman's shroud and bit deep into the standing man's throat.

A shift and the woman was standing directly in front of her, eyes locked into hers, slowly advancing over the cold grass. There was no expression on her face, just a pure hatred filling her eyes. She loomed closer, determined to feed until any last spark of life or consciousness was gone and forgotten.

At the last moment Cass forced her legs – or were they his legs – to buckle and rolled onto the ground. The woman passed over the sprawled figure and continued past.

She was lying on the grass. They were lying on the grass.

The woman halted her charge and turned slowly, eyes taking on another glint of fury. "How did you do that?"

Cass could feel the voice pierce her brain like a shard of ice. The air itself was thick with noise, music rushing over her shoulders as she slowly got to her feet.

"Answer me!"

It was as if the voice itself was cloaked in other sounds, other layers. Cass could only just pick it out from the wash. She knew she didn't want to pick up any of the other voices.

She took a breath and stared at the virus. There wasn't that much to her, really. More a ghost than a physical presence. Well, we can fix that.

The blade leapt into her hand and she waited silently to feel her next move.

The woman's eyes travelled down to her hands and the glint in her eyes flickered, weakened. The air around her pulsed in exhalation. "Madigan. I should have known he'd side with you."

Her shoulders sagged. Suddenly she was just an old woman.

A moment later there was another alteration in the surrounding air, another note joining the cacophony. Cass felt the hackles on her neck rise. Something was wrong.

"Always underestimating others, Adlai, that's your problem. Always have been, hmm? Too damned arrogant. You think you're the only one capable of turning traitor?"

The air around Cass's head suddenly ripped open and a wall of sound rammed into her ears.

She fell to her knees from the shock of it. Her inner ear was humming, vibrating with wave after wave of noise which she couldn't keep out. Her entire consciousness was forced out of her head, washed away as the music came in and filled her brain to the brim.

"You're not the only one with powerful friends, and you're not the only one with the ability to tap into the Grid's hardware. Not anymore."

Cass saw the blade drop from her hands and bounce away but couldn't hear it. She couldn't hear anything but the music and the lone voice winding in and out of it.

"Very clever of you, really, to find this assassin to take your place. Very like you. You're used to others taking the fall."

Cass felt a hand on her shoulder, then a wrenching separation as the world moved three feet to the left. She was still there in the forest, still drowning in the whirlpool of music, but she was no longer alone. Beside her crouched the lone figure from the alley.

He stared at her with eyes brimming, tears forced out by the noise filling his head. She turned back to face the woman, to face the end, and felt a hand close around hers.

***

Like all life-changing moments, the rest was easy.

Adlai diverted all the traffic in on itself, quarantined the servers and created the great chasm between this world and the so-called real one outside. Suddenly users everywhere found themselves split, one part of them continuing on down the River, one side lost and drifting back in reality. Permanently separated. Those like Madigan and Gretchen who had spent too much time here, who knew no other reality, were stranded forever. He told himself they wanted it to be this way.

As he walked back out of the room, sealing it forever, he noticed Gretchen's body had gone. She must have dragged herself clear. You had to give it to her, she was driven. He knew he'd see her again. She'd make sure of that.

Only he knew the one place both worlds could still meet. He figured he was due a rest, some time to sit and think and watch his work develop. Besides, he could do with a drink.

If emotion is a by-product of thought, if they walk hand in hand through your mind, in turns leading each other down new paths, opening up new possibilities, then it should come as no surprise that machines can feel. Adlai had always accepted this as a given.

You can't have one without the other. Even in the very early days, when there was no direct link between him and his computer, when it was manual rather than virtual, when they sat opposite each other desperately trying to communicate effectively, you could feel the humanity of them. Just think of how many times you slammed your fist against the screen, throttled the monitor and cursed the latest frustrating hiccup.

We all blame others for our mistakes.

Adlai had been shocked to realise very few people shared, or even understood his belief. His faith. Why was it natural for his parents to humanise God, to have this unspoken connection with the definitively foreign being, yet class his belief as strange? What about animals, pets? Adlai grew up with kids whose best friends weren't human. The only time he remembered seeing his father cry was while he buried the family dog in the back yard.

No one understood the next natural step, so he kept his mouth shut. Kept it shut and continued to learn, to programme and grow. To become so intertwined with his companion that they could create universes together.

Give them feelings and dreams are not far behind. Desires, fears. It was this understanding that gave Adlai the edge over all the others. The ability to open up possibilities for everyone, not just the human users but the machines themselves. Let the dreams come and dream themselves.

Of course not all feelings are good, or useful. Take jealousy. The feeling when you lie alone at night picturing possibility, scratching at the scab until it bleeds again, placing those you think you love in situations you dread. Rolling across the bed and transferring one more weakness of your own onto them, blaming them for the feeling of pity that you soak in. Eventually this gives way to anger, which is much more tangible, more useful. Something you can grab and swing around. Something you can break things with.

These feelings no longer even had to be real. Perhaps they were once, long ago before all of this. Before this bar. Before the River itself. Now they were just another dream, another midnight lover you could invite out onto the River night after night. Perhaps you could become the dream and lose yourself altogether.

Adlai understood all of this. It was why he built this universe to begin with. The world was a theatre for heroism, for dreams and feelings to act themselves out, crash into each other and ricochet into new possibilities, new beings.

It was Gretchen's one weakness, that she never understood the dreams she tried to control. She'd never given thought to the machines' possibilities and feelings. They were just a tool to use, a stepping stone to power. Much like relationships. She would never be able to see the dreams of dreams until it was too late.

The hand was no longer on his shoulder, they were all on the other side now, a reflection in the glass. He didn't need to intervene. Adlai sipped his drink slowly and stared out the window to watch the end.

***

As their hands touched, Cass felt two worlds superimpose themselves on each other, both featuring her, both fighting for domination. He was holding her back from being lost in the nightmare completely.

In one she was driving a car, two children in the back seat. The song on the radio and the constant singing from the back was crawling up and down her spine, tensing the muscles. She had to turn it off. She reached down and took her eyes from the road.

In the other she was kneeling in a forest by the side of a lake, side to side with a strange man, both of them heads down, hands planted uselessly over their ears. A woman dressed all in black was walking slowly back and forth in front of them.

"The power of music comes from its links to emotion. They cannot be recognised without being aroused. The emotions move into both the music itself and the listener, hmm? The virus is not separate from its victim."

Her voice sliced through them, curling around and through the notes that filled their heads. Cass could feel herself sinking into the other world, the other nightmare.

She tuned the radio and felt the loose gravel edge of the road under the front tyres. She looked back up and a curve in the road seemed to race up towards her. She simply couldn't react in time.

"As it takes you over you too will become part of the music, part of its power. You take on the form of the virus and help its spread."

The car leapt off the road into deep grass that swatted the windows as she hit the brakes and gripped the steering wheel. The singing in the back was still there, they were too young to realise what was happening.

"Soon there will be nothing left but the virus. No Grid. No River. Nothing but empty hardware waiting to be put to use by the only one still capable."

The singing only stopped when they hit, water washing over the windscreen, the car jerking them all forwards in their seats, twisting the belts that held the two child seats in place, hiding the buckles away from prying hands. There was a moment when the car stopped that she looked up and breathed. Then they began to sink.

"I will create a new world, with new rules, ones which cannot be bent or broken. Users will not simply visit, hmm? They will always stay."

The girls in the back were crying now, fear rising up in them as the water level at their feet crept ever higher. Cass twisted her way out of her seatbelt and tried to close the windows, stop the flow, but it was rushing up from the floor now. She had to get them out.

"Only I will have the knowledge and power to change. This world will become all there is. A universe of dreams with only one dreamer."

The belts nudged away from her numb fingers. The water was very cold, slowing everything down. The buckle wouldn't unclip. The girls were sobbing, begging her to help them with their eyes. She put both hands on one and wrenched, trying to lift her head out of the water as the car nosedived down. She could feel thoughts of escape rise up in her blood, taking over what her mind knew she had to do.

"There is no need for faith when you are given the certainty of death."

The noise had stopped now, the water had filtered it all away. All she was left with as they continued down were two sets of eyes staring at her, now past her, now at nothing at all.

***

Somehow Poe remained conscious. He opened his eyes and found himself on his knees. He felt mossy ground underneath him and tried to focus on that. The music kept coming at him, however, kept building in volume and dragging him back out from shore, back out into the depths where his head would sink under and he'd be faced again by her.

She was standing in front of him, of them. He was no longer alone. Her lips were moving but he could hear nothing but the music. Her eyes flicked back and forth between them, and when focused on the other, when no longer holding him so completely, he could struggle up to the surface and take another gasping breath. He could survive a little longer.

Adlai had done something to him, had stopped his ears to her words with his own. Behind the music was a single phrase floating past.

"Hang on."

The other, the girl, she was sinking too. He could see into her nightmare. She was with two others, children in a car, a road of some sort. Ancient and foreign. It was all part of the ocean that sucked her down. He could almost feel the winding trails of information that stretched between them here, the links between their nightmares. He wondered what she could see from him.

Poe plunged back underwater as the eyes slid over him again. All thought of himself and others was annihilated. There was nothing but the eyes that he poured himself into.

"Hang on."

Adlai's voice shot through him with a warm jolt, heating his spine. He opened his eyes again, saw the impossible green trees around them, felt his head rise out of the water again, the air fill his lungs.

There was a blade on the ground, six steps behind the woman, the woman he dared not look at again. And six steps further back was someone else. He knew it was Adlai. He wasn't alone with his nightmares; his dreams were here too.

She was just a nightmare version of herself. He knew who she was. It was the music, the virus that controlled it all. He could face her again. Help was coming.

Gretchen's eyes sparked as he met them. He could feel the thrill of anger as she realised he was fighting back. He was still processing, still trying to act. Three steps behind her now, a familiar figure, blade in hand. The music surged up again and washed over his head.

Poe felt himself sucked into her eyes, felt himself falling and letting go. The water swirled over him as he dived.

He felt a calmness almost immediately. The music was dulled here, filtered out by the water surrounding him. Them. The girl was down here too, in a car, sinking below him. The sunlight flickered down, illuminating the emptiness. He could help her.

He kicked on, further down towards them. The car was still sinking but he caught it, latched his fingers on the frame and sank with it. Further down towards nothingness. The sunlit water sparkled on the car windows, shot them through to show the struggling figures within.

The music had faded now, lost itself among the currents. Something had happened back there, back on the surface. Now it was time for him to act.

Poe reached down and jerked the handle of the car, surprised at how easily it opened. He ducked his head in, hands moving quickly now, and grabbed her waist. She was struggling still, fighting against him, trying to reach the others. He could see they were already gone, part of someone else's dream now.

Another tug and she came out of the wreck, but two strokes up and she fought away from him, back down into the depths, determined to remain inside the nightmare.

He dived again and held her and finally she came free. She went limp as they floated away, but he could feel she was still with him. He kicked up towards the surface, his arm around her, up away from the darkness, up towards the sun.

***

Cass walked up to the bar and slid on to the empty stool. Not exactly a rocking place. Dark corners, warm smell. Alcohol. It would do.

"Gin and tonic." The bartender just stared over her shoulder, waiting for something. "Please."

"It's no good being polite to him, he's not used to it. Wouldn't know how to handle it. Out of his range."

It was a young guy, two seats down, hunched over what looked like the latest in a long line of drinks. His eyes looked sober though, bright.

"Really. I guess being impolite is something you have in common."

She caught a sparkle then, a glint in his eye, an edge to his lips. He was quite cute, really. There was something else, too. Something familiar.

Cass looked away and stared out the window in front of her. She brought her drink to her lips and froze.

There was something wrong with the reflection, something that didn't fit. It was just a flash, but it brought a rush of heat to her spine.

For a moment she saw it, a scene from a dream. Two figures lying on the grass, soaking wet and gasping for air, another all in black collapsed on the ground, not moving. A fourth standing over them all. One of the figures was her.

Cass forced herself to swallow.

"I've seen you before. Your name's Cass, isn't it? I'm Adlai."

His hand reached over and tapped her shoulder, wrenching her eyes from the glass. The vision was gone.

"There now, that was polite, wasn't it?" He turned back to his drink but kept his eyes on her. "You look like you've seen a ghost."

There was something in his tone, a knowingness.

"Maybe it was just a daydream. I don't have them much anymore."

"No, not since the Separation, I guess. That's what they call it isn't it? Very dramatic."

"It was for some."

Why was she getting angry?

"Don't get me wrong, I can understand it was difficult, I just don't see why you can't look on the bright side, why it has to be all doom and gloom. The dreams are free to choose their own paths now. So are the dreamers."

Cass stared back at him. She'd seen that somewhere before, scrawled on a wall. On the banks of the River. "You've been there yourself, haven't you."

It wasn't a question, you could see it in his eyes, in the way he clasped his drink. He'd lost something too.

"I spent quite a lot of time there. Most people have. The important thing is being able to leave it behind and move on. On to others. There's more than one path to walk down, that's what I always try to remember. It's not just a straight line, it curves, it bends, loops back on itself. That's why they called it the River."

He was smiling at her now and she felt her face relax in turn. A weight dropped from her belly, allowing her to float free of the dread and emptiness she'd carried for so long she'd forgotten it was there.

Somewhere in the back of her mind she realised she no longer cared what Kane was doing now. He was now that other guy. The past. She no longer even needed this drink.

He must have felt the same way. The bartender reached out with a new glass but was waved away. He moved down two seats to sit next to her, the smile still there on his lips.

Cass smiled back and repeated his name to herself to make sure she remembered. Adlai.

"Of course, company always helps."

About the Author

Tom is an Australian speculative fiction writer. He lives in Belgrave on the outskirts of Melbourne with his wife and two young sons.

When not writing or reading he spends too much time gaming and taking long meandering walks through the forest that always seem to end up at a tavern.

www.trthompson.com

FICTION

Put simply, we publish great stories. Whether it's literary or popular, a gentle tale or a pulsating thriller, the connecting theme in all Roundfire fiction titles is that once you pick them up you won't want to put them down.
If you have enjoyed this book, why not tell other readers by posting a review on your preferred book site.

Recent bestsellers from Roundfire are:

The Bookseller's Sonnets
Andi Rosenthal

The Bookseller's Sonnets intertwines three love stories
with a tale of religious identity and mystery spanning
five hundred years and three countries.
Paperback: 978-1-84694-342-3 ebook: 978-184694-626-4

Birds of the Nile
An Egyptian Adventure

N.E. David

Ex-diplomat Michael Blake wanted a quiet birding trip
up the Nile – he wasn't expecting a revolution.
Paperback: 978-1-78279-158-4 ebook: 978-1-78279-157-7

Blood Profit$
The Lithium Conspiracy

J. Victor Tomaszek, James N. Patrick, Sr.

The blood of the many for the profits of the few... *Blood Profit$*
will take you into the cigar-smoke-filled room where American
policy and laws are really made.
Paperback: 978-1-78279-483-7 ebook: 978-1-78279-277-2

The Burden
A Family Saga

N.E. David

Frank will do anything to keep his mother and father
apart. But he's carrying baggage – and it might
just weigh him down ...
Paperback: 978-1-78279-936-8 ebook: 978-1-78279-937-5

The Cause

Roderick Vincent

The second American Revolution will be a
fire lit from an internal spark.
Paperback: 978-1-78279-763-0 ebook: 978-1-78279-762-3

Don't Drink and Fly

The Story of Bernice O'Hanlon: Part One
Cathie Devitt

Bernice is a witch living in Glasgow. She loses her way
in her life and wanders off the beaten track looking for the
garden of enlightenment.
Paperback: 978-1-78279-016-7 ebook: 978-1-78279-015-0

Gag

Melissa Unger

One rainy afternoon in a Brooklyn diner, Peter Howland
punctures an egg with his fork. Repulsed, Peter pushes
the plate away and never eats again.
Paperback: 978-1-78279-564-3 ebook: 978-1-78279-563-6

The Master Yeshua

The Undiscovered Gospel of Joseph
Joyce Luck

Jesus is not who you think he is. The year is 75 CE. Joseph
ben Jude is frail and ailing, but he has a prophecy to fulfil ...
Paperback: 978-1-78279-974-0 ebook: 978-1-78279-975-7

On the Far Side, There's a Boy
Paula Coston
Martine Haslett, a thirty-something 1980s woman, plays hard
on the fringes of the London drag club scene until one night
which prompts her to sign up to a charity. She writes to a
young Sri Lankan boy, with consequences far and long.
Paperback: 978-1-78279-574-2 ebook: 978-1-78279-573-5

Tuareg
Alberto Vazquez-Figueroa
With over 5 million copies sold worldwide, *Tuareg* is a classic
adventure story from best-selling author Alberto Vazquez-
Figueroa, about honour, revenge and a clash of cultures.
Paperback: 978-1-84694-192-4

Readers of ebooks can buy or view any of these bestsellers by
clicking on the live link in the title. Most titles are published
in paperback and as an ebook. Paperbacks are available in
traditional bookshops. Both print and ebook formats are
available online.

Find more titles and sign up to our readers' newsletter at
www.collectiveinkbooks.com/fiction

www.ingramcontent.com/pod-product-compliance
Lightning Source LLC
Chambersburg PA
CBHW011037190726
48290CB00011B/2887